The Trouble with Jacob

The Trouble with Jacob

ELOISE McGRAW

Margaret K. McElderry Books

NEW YORK

Margaret K. McElderry Books
Macmillan Publishing Company
866 Third Avenue
New York, NY 10022
Collier Macmillan Canada, Inc.

Composition by Maryland Linotype Composition Company
Baltimore, Maryland

Designed by Barbara A. Fitzsimmons

First Edition

Printed in the United States of America

10   9   8   7   6   5   4   3   2   1

Library of Congress Cataloging-in-Publication Data

McGraw, Eloise Jarvis.
The trouble with Jacob.

Summary: Twelve-year-old twins Andy and Kat think
they are in for a dull summer at a remote resort in
western Oregon, until the ghost of a nine-year-old boy
appears demanding restitution for a crime committed
over 100 years before.
[1. Ghosts—Fiction. 2. Twins—Fiction. 3. Oregon—
Fiction] I. Title.
PZ7.M47853Tr   1988   [Fic]   87-22719
ISBN 0-689-50447-0

For Peter, Milena and Patrick

The Trouble with Jacob

CHAPTER ONE

Andy Peterson first set eyes on the boy around two o'clock of a Wednesday afternoon, on a sunny hillside—a time and place that seemed as strange, when he looked back on it, as the boy himself. Stranger still was the fact that he'd paid so little attention, right there at the beginning, either to the boy or what he said. He'd been curious—anybody would be. And surely anybody might have guessed that something peculiar was going on.

The fact remained that Andy hadn't. Too busy gawking around the unfamiliar Hidden Creek countryside, trying not to miss anything. And Kat had been busy listening to a tape and probably thinking about something back in Portland, or ahead to her brilliant future on the concert stage. Their usual totally opposite reactions to a sudden shift of scene. It was really no wonder people never believed the Peterson kids were twins; they were about as much alike as a sparrow and an owl. Andy was surprised, himself, at how well they usually got along.

This particular Wednesday was near the end

of June, only a week or so after he and Kat had arrived with their mother, Dodie, on very short notice, to spend their summer running Hidden Creek Lodge, Uncle Richard's resort/retreat half-way up an Oregon mountain. They had arrived because Uncle Richard's partner and best friend, Todd, had decamped the previous week on no notice at all, taking the VCR and every penny in sight.

Uncle Richard had phoned Portland the next morning. "You've got to come. I've got to get away," he'd kept repeating mournfully to Dodie, drowning out her protests that she had a summer French conversation class to teach, that the twins had plans. "I've just *got* to get away, and sort things out, and lick my wounds and all. I mean, it *hurts*. In all the world I've got only my savings and this Lodge."

"Well, you shouldn't have let him rob you blind," Dodie said exasperatedly.

"—and no friends, only a wonderful, loving sister who's never let me down."

Of course she'd eventually given in, rearranged their summer at great inconvenience to every-body, and here they were, the three of them, in sole charge of Hidden Creek Lodge—temporarily. "*Very* temporarily," she had told Uncle Richard in her most ferocious voice, when they'd dropped their suitcases in the Lodge's lobby, and he'd picked his up. "You listen to me, Richard. If you're not back by mid-August it's going to be just too bad—for your Lodge and your employees and whatever paying guests happen to be staying here at the time—because that's when the kids and I go back to town!" He was her younger brother; she could talk to him that way—the way she talked to her students at Campion Hall.

Unlike her students, he remained uncowed, merely sighing. "Cool it, Dodie, I'm only going to Japan." He then smiled a sad good-bye to all of them and went away.

Kat said uneasily, "He *will*, won't he, Dodie? Be back by mid-August? Because I'm *scheduled* for the final week of music camp and if I'm late or anything they'll probably never *consider* me again, and—"

"You heard him—he's only going to Japan," said Dodie, rolling her eyes as she always did about Uncle Richard but also grinning a little. "You heard what *I* said, too—and you may consider that a promise. Andy, pick up those bags and let's get over to the cottage and get unpacked."

So they'd got unpacked, and settled in, and started learning how to run the Lodge. It took a lot of behind-the-scenes action just to keep it in working order, whether there was a group coming to stay or not. Andy's job had turned out to be grounds maintenance, he alone having the size and heft for it. This chiefly meant fighting off the forest, which kept trying to grow back over the front clearing and the parking area and the few nature trails Uncle Richard had managed to establish. It also meant supplying wood for both the big handsome fireplace in the Lodge and the small smoky one in Uncle Richard's rustic cottage at the far end of the clearing, where the Petersons were living. Since Dodie had her hands full overseeing the large main building and the row of ten additional sleeping cabins known as The Annex, Kat took charge of the cottage. In between her rather slapdash duties there, she practiced scales and finger exercises on the old foot-pumped organ Uncle Richard had bought somewhere and installed on the open balcony overlooking the Lodge's lounge—chiefly to fill space and look quaint. As she reported to Andy, it was a mile from being a piano, but if you didn't touch the pedals it made no sound, and you were invisible unless somebody happened to look up, which wasn't often. She could put in three hours a day on silent Czerny exercises—though she fretted about her Bach.

Not exactly a restful holiday for anybody.

"If we weren't here," Kat told Andy moodily as she trailed him out the door that Wednesday afternoon, "I'd have that fugue half memorized. Or at least be listening to live music somewhere instead of these same old tapes." She hooked her tape player over her belt with a grouchy jerk.

Andy couldn't blame her. "Yeah. *I* might be out sailing on Phil's dad's boat." His mind went on supplying things he could be doing at home in Portland: reading half the day if he wanted to, finishing the spice shelf he'd been making for Dodie for going on two years now, biking across town to see his friend Mr. Cummings, who was the reptile keeper at the zoo, or out to the nursing home to talk to Great-Aunt Madge and all the old odd-balls she knew there. They were really interesting, some of those old people, if you just got them talking and *listened*. His friend Phil Darling thought he was crazy for liking to go out there. Phil had gone along with Andy once—just once. He'd asked to. But once was enough, he'd said after that, rolling his eyes whenever Andy mentioned it. Phil liked things to be happening all the time— the same as Kat. Neither one of them was willing to just sit there and watch, and listen, and wonder about people.

Oh, well. They *weren't* in Portland. Right this minute, they were on their way to nearby Harper's Mill, he with his empty backpack slung over his shoulder, to pick up the mail and five dozen eggs. There was a writer's group coming to the lodge on Friday for the weekend.

"We'll survive," he told Kat—adding reasonably, "After all, you've got to help out your own relatives. Uncle Richard was all shook up."

"He could've *hired* somebody to take over. Somebody who'd already worked at the Lodge— like about half the people in Harper's Mill. Somebody who knew how to run it."

"We'll know how to run it pretty soon." Andy veered off toward the rear of the clearing. "Let's take the shortcut."

They'd already discovered that the quickest way to the town was the back way, right over the ridge behind the Lodge and steeply down through forest and ferns and tangles of vine maple until you emerged onto open hillside above the little pioneer graveyard. The slope eased to a gentler angle there, and you could turn across it on a sort of cow path which ran alongside the cemetery fence to its corner. Then you were on Mr. Harry Buckle's property and could follow his graveled lane on down between his slanting hay fields and the wooded shoulder of the hill until you hit the paved county road into town.

If you could call Harper's Mill a town. Dodie called it "the village," but she favored interesting names for things. Skiers driving through on their way up the mountain probably thought of it as that wide spot in the highway just before you reached the turnoff to Sugar Meadows. But it *was* a town, with a post office and a supermarket and so on—you just couldn't see it all from the highway.

Andy could see it now—at least its cluster of roofs—as he followed the faint tinselly sound escaping from Kat's earphones down the cow path and onto the crunchy gravel of the Buckles' lane. You could see half of Oregon from here. The forested hill rising at his right hand was part of the Cascade Range.

He turned to glance that way and saw the boy standing among the shadows at the edge of the trees—a skinny little kid, towheaded. Andy judged him a couple of years younger than himself, maybe nine or ten. His expression was wary, as if he were a deer waiting to see if Andy had a gun. It was the way a lot of the kids around here looked at Kat and him.

In Andy's opinion it was a dumb way to act, but he halfway waved at the boy. Nobody was going to say the city kids up at the Lodge were trying to upstage anybody.

The boy didn't respond, nor did his expression change. But, surprisingly, he turned and began to keep pace with them down the hill, still staying just within the shadow of the trees. It was the nearest to a friendly overture any local kid had yet made.

Andy glanced ahead at Kat to see if she'd noticed, but of course she hadn't; the earphones were still in place. He could see the gleam of the headband arching above her thick red braid like a sort of misplaced halo. She was playing an imaginary piano in the air in front of her, and looking toward the valley—probably watching Mr. Buckle's big Belgian mares lumbering after their energetic colts in the lower pasture. Glancing back toward the boy, Andy found he could no longer see him among the trees. But an instant later he spotted him a dozen yards ahead, emerging hesitantly into a hillside clearing that overlooked the lane. He was awfully fast on his feet—or else part grasshopper. In either case it might mean friendly interest. Producing a smile that felt as if he'd borrowed it from somebody else, Andy called "Hi," as he came abreast of the clearing.

The boy halted immediately and said "Hiyuh," in a soft, ragged-edged little voice that sounded as if he had a touch of laryngitis. Andy stopped, too. Before he could think of another remark the boy said something else Andy didn't quite catch. Something urgent.

"What?" Andy asked, stepping toward the bank that formed the uphill side of the lane.

The boy repeated it, with the same urgency: "Somebody's got my bed!"

Andy stared at him, wondering how he was supposed to react to this message, which was as unexpected as if it had been delivered in Swahili. As a conversation killer it ranked right up there at the top.

He was just beginning, "Whaddya mean?" when Kat called back to him, from down the lane.

"Hey, come on! Dodie said. . . . Who're you talking to?"

He turned to find her starting back toward him, pulling her earphones down around her neck and squinting curiously toward the hillside.

"That kid there," Andy told her, with a sideways jerk of his head.

"What kid?"

Andy looked back toward the clearing. The boy had disappeared again—probably behind that big rock thrusting up through the underbrush near the woods' edge. Or maybe just behind a tree. The wary deer act again.

"Hey!" Andy called. "Hey, come on back, it's only my sister." No response. No sign that anybody had ever been there. Andy frowned, trying to recapture some impression that had caught on the tip of his mind. Some detail—of appearance? Of speech? Something besides the urgency. Then he gave up and started on. "There was a boy up there a minute ago. I guess he left."

"Down a rabbit hole?" Kat inquired, after a brief inspection of the woods.

"Well, he's probably hiding."

"Hiding? Why?" Kat snapped off her tape player, ready to be intrigued.

"How do I know? Maybe he's scared of girls."

"Oh, c'*mon*."

"Look, you didn't miss a thing. He was just a weirdo."

"Weirdo? Way out here?"

"No, no . . ." Andy didn't know why he'd said that. Except to stop Kat's questions, which for some reason made him uncomfortable. "Not the city kind of weirdo. Just a—sort of oddball little kid."

"So what did he want? I mean, what did he say?"

Andy sighed. A mosquito gave up quicker than his sister Katherine. Patiently, he answered her. "He told me somebody'd got his bed."

"Got his *bed*?"

"That's what it sounded like."

"But what did he mean? They stole it?"

"I don't know. He sounded awful worried."

"But—"

"Look, that's all I know!"

So even Kat, after puzzling a moment, gave up.

The incident seemed meaningless, no matter how many ways you looked at it. Maybe some kind of joke that didn't come off. Andy glanced back once more at the empty hillside, reminded himself that little kids were always talking nonsense and then expecting you to know exactly what they meant, ignored the inner voice that told him *this* kid wasn't all that little, and ended by advising himself emphatically to forget it.

And at that moment, he was sure he would. He changed the subject. "Did Dodie say we should get white eggs this time?" he asked before Kat could get her earphones back in place.

"I don't think she said."

"Let's do. They're cheaper."

"Brown eggs are *richer*, though."

"Hah. Who says?"

"Mrs. Corey. The Mrs. Corey who cooks."

"I *know* which one," Andy told her. There was also a youngish Mrs. Corey, chambermaid in The Annex, who never seemed to talk at all. Mrs. Corey-who-cooked never stopped.

"Well, she won't like it if we get white. She says Uncle Richard always bought the *best* for the Lodge."

"I'll bet Uncle Richard didn't have the foggiest idea what color eggs he was buying. Anyhow, Todd was doing the buying."

"That's right," Kat said. She added sadly, "Probably buying white and charging him for brown. *Why* did it take Uncle Richard so long to catch on?"

"Beats me. I suppose since such a thing never *had* happened to him, he just figured it never would." It struck Andy that he might have hit on some kind of real deep truth there, about Uncle Richard. It did not strike him—until much later—that Uncle Richard had no copyright on blindfold reasoning.

"I'll bet that was it," Kat was agreeing. "Look at us. *We* never thought we'd be running a lodge—or thinking of Harper's Mill as 'downtown.' "

"Oh, Harper's Mill's not bad," Andy said peaceably. "Admit it. If we weren't always wishing it was Portland, we'd think it was a pretty nice place."

The *place* wasn't really the problem, he mused as they crunched on down the lane. They all three liked the Lodge, and Andy supposed that if he and Kat ever got time to explore the Hidden Creek area, they'd like that, too. But there seemed nobody of their age within reach. The few kids who lived in the town itself were mostly younger, or involved with jobs; the rest were scattered far and wide on the surrounding farms, and with school out, apparently found no reason to leave home—certainly not just to make friends with the newcomers.

"They probably go see each *other*," remarked Kat, who had obviously been on the same train of thought. "And go swimming and have picnics and stuff. They must. They're all related."

"Not all," Andy objected.

"They *are*. Everybody around Harper's Mill is

at least cousins or in-laws with everybody else. If their name isn't Harper, it's Corey or Sweet."

"What about Harry Buckle?" Andy jerked his head toward the Buckles' driveway, the entrance to which had just appeared on their left through the lane-side screen of wild hazel.

Kat gave him a look that disposed of quibbling, and transferred her earphones from around her neck to over her ears, snapping her tape back on. However, she, too, glanced down the short, rutted drive toward the open space Andy supposed should be called a barnyard. It did have two big barns ranged along one side of it, and on the other a shed and a stretch of green lawn shaded by an enormous maple. At the far end, a white farmhouse half hid its face behind a veil of flowering vine. The first day they'd walked by here they'd seen one of the huge Belgian draft horses being led into a barn, looking like some Superhorse meant for a Super-knight in full armor; another time they'd glimpsed some sort of fancy equipage, painted red and glittering with brass, through the open doors of the other barn. This time they saw Harry Buckle himself, a burly, gray-haired man of fifty-odd, crossing the barnyard toward the house.

He saw them, too, and stopped. "Hi, there. How you doing?" he said genially.

Andy murmured something, trying to pretend he

hadn't been gawking like a sightseer. Kat raised one earphone.

"You're the kids from up at the Lodge, aren't you? I got that right?"

"Yessir."

"Richard Carpenter's kinfolks." Mr. Buckle ambled toward them. "Your name Carpenter, too?"

"Peterson," Kat broke in, turning her tape off and hanging the earphones on her belt. A little friendliness and she opened like a flower spreading its petals to the sun. "We're Anders and Katherine Peterson."

"Andy and Kat," Andy translated hastily.

"Mighty glad to make your acquaintance, Andy and Kat." Mr. Buckle extended a large, callused hand, which enveloped each of theirs in turn. "I'm friends with a lot of the youngsters around here. They come to see my Belgians, not me, but can't blame 'em for that. I teach 'em to drive."

"You let *kids* drive those great big horses?" Kat said in astonishment.

"Sure. Got a 4-H group comes every week. I'll teach *you* to drive 'em if you like." Mr. Buckle grinned and added, "Want to meet Bonnie and Clyde? Come on. I'll introduce you."

He started toward the farthest barn, and after a quick exchange of glances, Kat and Andy followed. So if they were a little late with the eggs, who'd care, except maybe Mrs. Corey-who-cooked?

"Got one or two kids your size driving pretty good already," Mr. Buckle told Kat as he led the way across the hard-packed ground. "You must be ten, eleven?"

"We're twelve and a half," Kat told him.

Now it was Mr. Buckle who looked startled, as he glanced from her to Andy. "What, both of you?"

"Well, I'm fifteen minutes older. We're twins," Andy said, and braced himself for the usual reaction to this news. He realized it was hard to believe. Kat was small boned, foxy colored and wiry, like Dodie. He was white-blond, built on truck driver lines, and always being taken for several years older than his friends. *Another great, big, IMMOVABLE Swede*, Dodie was apt to call him under her breath in her more astringent moods. He assumed he took after his father, whom he could only distantly remember as a fair-haired giant waving good-bye from a bus—a permanent good-bye, Andy knew now, from his wife and children.

Mr. Buckle was not reacting in quite the usual manner—which was to stare at Andy as if he were somehow gross and should in all decency shrink down to nearer sixth-grade size. Instead, he turned to slide open the tall barn door, smiling a little, as if at some picture in his mind. "I had twin cousins, back in Texas where I grew up," he remarked. "At your age, one was about six foot two and the other five one. They never had a thought in common in their lives."

Andy, who was pushing five eleven himself, relaxed and said he and Kat actually shared quite a few. He was deciding he liked Mr. Buckle a lot.

And *he* might know who that oddball kid is, thought Andy suddenly.

But right now Kat was asking a lot of questions about the 4-H group. And a minute later they went in the barn, and Andy forgot all about the boy on the hillside because he fell in love.

CHAPTER TWO

Bonnie and Clyde were a matched team of Belgians—the first Andy had ever seen up close. They stood in neighboring stalls, hanging their big, flaxen-maned heads over the half doors from what seemed an immense height for a domestic animal. Their tails were flaxen, too—long and sweeping, he saw when Mr. Buckle led Bonnie out into the center aisle—and their vast, shiny coats nearly copper. Bonnie's white-blazed nose—its velvety, whiskery tip—was about even with Andy's own, and her front hoof, clomping hollowly past him on the worn wooden floor, looked as if it would barely fit into a milk bucket. Her eyes, as she swung her massive head down to look him over, were dark, long lashed, and gently curious. Andy looked back at her and lost his heart.

"She's my best girl," said Mr. Buckle, giving a resounding slap to the golden shoulder, which topped his own. "My lead horse, too—the boss. She tells ol' Clyde where to get off when he isn't pulling his half of the load."

"She's sure a beauty," Andy muttered, reaching up to stroke her shoulder himself. It radiated warmth, and felt like a satin-covered rock. Just imagine *owning* a horse like that, Andy thought. Getting to look at her every day . . . and giving her oats, and doing whatever else it is you do for horses . . . well, sure, cleaning her stall, I wouldn't mind that a *bit*—and bringing her water, and driving her, and maybe riding . . .

Kat, who had her head tilted as far back as it would go, was apparently struck dumb by the size of the creature before her and for once said nothing at all.

"D'you ride a horse that big?" Andy ventured.

"Oh, you can climb on to get from here to there, but not serious riding, no. A draft horse is built to pull."

"How much do they weigh, anyhow?" Andy asked in awe.

"They vary. This pair's right around twenty-two hundred apiece last time I checked."

"*Pounds?*" Kat said almost inaudibly.

Andy added, trying to believe it, "That's a ton."

"A little over. And all sweet temper. My Bonnie's a great gal." Mr. Buckle led Bonnie in a dignified, clomping circle and restored her to her stall, gave a rough knuckling of the forelock to Clyde, who had thrust his head out jealously, then found them each a carrot. Much too soon, he led the way back out of the barn.

Andy followed with great reluctance. "D'you drive them often?" he asked.

"You bet I do. They'll be working pretty soon. Some kids coming for a birthday party wagon ride. You got time to stick around?"

"Oh, wow!" Kat was beginning, eyes and petals both opening wide, but Andy suddenly came to.

"Oh. No. Thanks—but we better get going. We're supposed to be getting the mail. I mean . . . Anyhow, if it's a party . . ."

Kat closed up like a prodded sea anemone. "Yeah, we wouldn't want to butt in."

Mr. Buckle shrugged and said, "The more the merrier," but Kat was already edging toward the lane, and Andy followed, walking backwards. "Thanks anyway," he added. "And thanks for showing us Bonnie and Clyde. Maybe we could— have a rain check?"

"Pleasure. Drop in any time." Harry Buckle smiled, gave a half salute, and went on his interrupted way to the house.

That sounded like a rain check to Andy. He stowed it carefully in a mental pocket, like diamonds in the bank.

"*Imagine* riding in a wagon behind those horses!" Kat sighed as they walked on down the lane. "Like a queen! Like the Queen of England in that golden coach!"

"But a birthday party, Kat!"

Reluctantly, she nodded. "Yeah. A whole bunch of kids all named Corey or Sweet or Harper—probably all wishing we'd go away."

"Give 'em time, they'll learn to love us yet," Andy murmured. He didn't care so much about the birthday party wagon ride. What he was thinking of was that 4-H group—and not just riding behind the horses, but maybe actually, unbelievably, driving them himself. Harder to imagine than the Queen of England's coach—but Mr. Buckle looked like a man who meant what he said.

Once they reached the end of the Buckles' lane and headed down the county road, it was only half a mile to the edge of Harper's Mill. They went first to the post office, an aggressively new one, with a circular drive and landscaping and a tall flagpole in front, as ill-suited to the rest of the dim little town as a bright-flowered hat on a bag lady. Andy went to the window to collect the Lodge mail from the postmaster—predictably, a Mr. Harper—and stowed it in his backpack while Kat opened their own personal box on the wall. They met again on their way out the door, Kat handing over a post-card.

"From Phil. He's having a great time sailing and wishes you were there."

"Thanks a *lot* for reading my mail to me."

"Don't mention it," Kat said airily.

He studied the card, wondering if he, too, still wished he were there. Well, maybe. But things might be picking up around here, what with Bonnie and Clyde and that weird little kid with his lost bed.

I forgot to ask Mr. Buckle about that kid. The moment he had the thought, Andy's mind was full of the boy's thin, worried face and peculiar problem, and the quite unreasonable notion that he, Andy Peterson, should be doing something about them. But what? he demanded unanswerably of the busy interior voice that was scolding him, and pointed out that he didn't even know what the problem was all about. *Well, something!* insisted the voice, illogical but stubborn. *At least find out who he is.* Irritably Andy promised he'd try, and the voice faded away as Kat's took over, telling him to quit blocking the doorway.

Sliding Phil's card into his hip pocket, he moved outside. "Want a coke before we start back?"

"Well, I'm *thirsty*," Kat admitted. But she hesitated, staring glumly across the street at Harper's Supermarket—the only grocery store in town. It was owned by the same Mr. Leonard Harper who owned the poultry farm, and it was operated by his wife. Early on, Kat had taken one of her strong dislikes to both of them.

"We've got no choice," Andy pointed out. "Come on, she won't bite."

They had to wait around a few minutes pretending interest in the cabbage display because the big
refrigerator was under siege by a rabble of Cub
Scouts all trying to get cold drinks at once. Swiftly
—and despite common sense—Andy searched the
group for his little towhead of the woods, telling
himself all the while that no kid could have raced
down here and joined the Scouts this quick, however fast he moved. Anyway, these were just
ordinary kids. As they streamed by on their way
to the checkout stand—each one giving Andy a
solemn stare—he wondered again what it was that
had made the boy on the hill seem *un*ordinary. He
couldn't pin it down.

"Okay, our turn," Kat said, giving him a shove.

They made their purchase, as usual creating a
lull in the checkout-line conversation, moved past
Mrs. Harper's perfunctory smile and eagle eye, and
finally, out the door.

Andy took a long, refreshing swig of his coke
and shrugged away the sensation of having been
under a spotlight. "Just curious, probably. Trying
to decide if they believe we're twins. Or maybe it's
just they don't see many strangers."

"It's just they don't have many manners," Kat
said crossly as they started on. "I wish we didn't
have to get our eggs from the Harpers, too—it's
bad enough trading at their store."

"I'll do the egg-buying, if you want. Shall we ask for white?"

"It's all right with me. But what if Mrs. Corey-who-cooks sends us right back for brown?"

"Dodie'll handle *her*," Andy said confidently. "Anyhow, she couldn't really care."

"Well, I don't know. That Mr. Leonard Harper is her brother-in-law!" Kat thought a minute, sipping her coke. "You know what? I'll bet she was *in* that scam with Todd! If he was buying white right along and *charging* Uncle Richard for brown—"

"Kat—we just made that up ourselves."

"—and Mr. Leonard Harper was in it, too. . . . Oh, quit laughing! It *might* be true."

"Well, we'll work on it," Andy promised. He believed in waiting till crises arrived before getting all uptight. Kat liked to bring them on. He then unwittingly paved the way for the next one by adding comfortably, "Why worry? There's probably other places to get eggs."

Kat said she doubted it, and retired, grumbling, into her earphones as they climbed the sloping street.

Harper's Poultry Farm marked the upper edge of town, where the little grid of streets gave way to the fields and scattered houses bordering the county road. Unlike the brisk, cheerful Mr. Edwin

Harper who was the postmaster, Mr. Leonard
Harper was a thin, sour-looking man with a bald
spot and a prominent Adam's apple who spoke,
when necessary, in monosyllables, and in Andy's
opinion deserved the pickle-faced wife he had got.
While he went to get their order, Kat kept her
earphones on and stood absolutely still, disdain-
fully scanning the untidy yard, where a number of
unofficial chickens stalked about making their own
living, pecking desultorily and croaking long-
drawn questions at each other, meanwhile leaving
their droppings everywhere and feather-fluff on
every weed. Andy had to agree, L. Harper's was
not precisely the last word in modern cleanliness.
He hoped the eggs were fresh.

He paid for them, stuffed the fat bundle of
cartons into his pack, and said, "Thanks a lot."

Mr. Harper walked away.

"*Really!*" Kat exploded the minute they were
out of earshot. "Who does he think he is, anyhow?"

"Somebody lots better'n us," Andy told her.
"More like George Washington, or maybe Johnny
Appleseed. His great-great-grandaddy probably
cleared that land he's on. Dodie said there's some
real old families around here. Descendants of
pioneers, and all that."

"I don't care if they're descendants of Lewis and
Clark! They could be polite." Scowling, Kat re-

adjusted her earphones and abruptly retreated into a tape.

Andy, who had opened his mouth to reply, closed it again and mused briefly on the politeness of ending a conversation in that particular way—it was as if she'd stepped into a closet and slammed the door. Phil did it all the time too, so Andy was used to it. Nothing personal. She only wanted the familiar comfort of some music—any music; she liked all kinds.

Walking beside her, a few paces away, he listened idly to the faint jingle coming from her earphones. It always sounded like tiny tambourines being played in the middle distance—or maybe from high above, at about church steeple level. This was some rock group, probably; he thought he could identify the rhythm. As they approached the turn into the Buckles' lane he was just making a small bet with himself that it was either the Light Bulbs, or—

Kat pushed the earphones down around her neck. "Hey, Andy! You know something?"

"Say, what was that?" Andy asked her interestedly.

"What was what?"

"Tape. The Light Bulbs, right?. Or was it The Dregs?"

Kat rolled her eyes and said, "Mozart. Will you listen to what I'm saying?"

"Oh. Yeah, sure. Go on." He was no good at music anyway.

"Well, look, we could get our eggs from Mr. Buckle! Couldn't we? He's *lots* nicer than that old stuck-up—"

"Does Mr. Buckle sell eggs?"

"I'll bet he does. He's got those great big chicken houses over there. See? Just downhill from his house."

"Oh, yeah." Both of them peered across the lane-side thickets toward the two long, low structures. They certainly *looked* like chicken houses— and there was a big fenced run between them. "We could ask Dodie about it," Andy said.

"Let's do! I'd love to spit in that rude old Mr. Harper's eye."

Andy laughed but made no comment. It did occur to him that to switch the Lodge account to a competitor just because Kat wanted to spit in Mr. Leonard Harper's eye might not be ideal behavior for newcomers. As Dodie would no doubt inform them. No use to make enemies, he reflected. But he had had so little experience with enemies that he forgot the thought almost before he had it. His next one was far more interesting.

"We better find out first if they really have eggs to sell," he remarked, thinking *rain check*. "Should we stop in now?"

"That birthday party might be there."

But nobody was in sight in the Buckles' barnyard, not even the birds whose calls criss-crossed it incessantly in the sunlit air. Either the birthday party hadn't arrived yet or had already come and gone. If the latter, Mr. Buckle *might* be in the house.

"C'mon," Andy said. He stashed his backpack out of sight under a hazel bush, and they turned again into the hard-rutted drive.

Diffidently they walked past both barns, past the big maple opposite, toward the white house at the far end of the barnyard. The vine that veiled the old-fashioned front porch was parted primly in the middle to reveal the doorway and a woman sitting on a kitchen chair in front of it. She was a comfortably shaped woman wearing a pale pink cardigan that contrasted oddly with her worn cowboy boots, and she was surrounded by baskets and bowls of strawberries. Her capable hands went right on stemming the fruit as she greeted them.

"Now, don't tell me, let me see if I can guess," she began immediately, peering over her half-glasses to fix them with a bright blue gaze. "The new kids from up at the Lodge—that right? The hard-to-believe twins. Name's Anderson."

"Peterson," Andy corrected her. "Andy and Kat."

"Well, I did pretty good—for me. I'm Myra Buckle. Have a strawberry. Just pick up a handful from anywhere. What can I do for you? Or did you want to see Harry?"

"I'm not sure," Andy said. "We came about eggs."

"We wondered if Mr. Buckle sells them," Kat explained. "We saw those big chicken houses—or whatever they are—"

"Oh, that's what they are," Mrs. Buckle assured her. "But Harry only sells Belgians—he's busy now anyway," she added to Andy's disappointment. "You want my brother Ellerton—he lives with us. He's the egg man around here."

"Does he have brown eggs or white eggs?" Kat demanded.

"Brown, white, speckled, maybe a few pink and green ones," said Mrs. Buckle. "If a thing grows feathers, Ellerton's feedin' it. He's right in the living room. You wanta talk to him? *Ellerton!*" she yelled before they could answer, then went on, "Lemme just warn you—he's a little deaf. You'll hardly notice—I keep forgettin' it myself, he's so good at lip-reading. But be sure he's looking at you when you talk to him, less'n you want to screech ever'thing you say. Ellerton?" she said with a questioning glance over her shoulder. "Come on out and meet your new customers—it's those twins Harry was telling us about."

The screen door behind her opened, and a slight, stooped man of about Dodie's age came out.

"Twins, hm?" he said in a soft, tranquil voice. "My g'ness, you don't even hardly look related, do you? That's innerestin'."

He meant it, too, Andy could tell from the way he looked from one to the other of them as he came forward to offer his hand to each in turn. He had a thin, unremarkable face set with greenish eyes that somehow held your attention, and a smile that was like the sun coming out. Kat was already opening her petals in response to it, explaining that they *wanted* to be customers, but had to get permission first.

"Well, I understand that. Sure I do. I'll run down to my office, get you a price list to show your ma. How'd you like to come along, see my poultry house?"

"Okay!" Kat agreed before Andy could open his mouth. "I bet yours is cleaner than Mr. Harper's," she confided, as readily as if she and Ellerton had been friends for years.

"Oh, I hear that Harper place is a caution," said Ellerton with a sad shake of his head.

They started off chummily together around the corner of the house, and before he followed them Andy exchanged a glance with Mrs. Buckle, who grinned and shrugged, and gave him another handful of strawberries. Ellerton's shyness-dissolving charm was evidently nothing new to her.

At the back of the house, the Buckles' property

fell away toward the county road. There a path curved downward between a burgeoning vegetable garden and a stretch of slanting pasture, in the direction of the two long roofs the twins had seen from the lane. Andy caught up with Kat and Ellerton at the minimal wire fence edging the pasture, where they had stopped to look down the grassy slope. About halfway down, near a huge spreading tree, half a dozen or so of the big Belgians were milling around, chasing each other in little circles, nipping and half rearing, pausing only occasionally to snatch absentminded bites of grass.

"They look like they're *playing*," Andy said in astonishment as he stopped to watch too.

"Yeah. They're only five-year-olds," Ellerton told him. "Belgians don't get to be grown-ups till they're six. 'Course these're as big as their daddies already, but they don't know it. Jes' look at 'em. Bouncin' around as if they was still half that size."

Andy *was* looking, with some apprehension. At the sound of voices the whole troop had started uphill at an all-out gallop, hooves thundering, ears pricked; roughly six tons of stampeding horseflesh converging on three lone humans at top speed. In spite of himself Andy stepped back; Kat was already behind him.

"They'll stop," Ellerton assured them serenely. "That there fence is electric."

They did stop, colliding with one another, just

short of the two fragile wires—about one inch short of it, Andy judged, looking almost straight up at the tossing heads. For a moment the world seemed full of flying white manes and tails and dust and throaty whufflings. Then the whole bunch wheeled and took off, nipping at each other's flanks, dodging, kicking up their heels, only to swirl back a moment later to the fence again.

"Buncha rowdy big teenagers," Ellerton said indulgently.

"Rowdy is right," Kat muttered with a last glance over her shoulder as they turned away to walk on down the path.

They heard the poultry house before they saw it—a continuous high-pitched din that didn't sound like any kind of bird Andy had ever heard. It was more like a sort of jingling, shrieking, mechanical noise. Like a rusty iron-wheeled cart, he decided, hung with small dangling chains and full of excited first-graders going *very slowly* to a picnic. He was about to share this vision with Kat when a last little rise in the undulating path revealed the fenced enclosure between the sheds, and the source of the racket.

"Guinea hens," explained Ellerton.

"Is that what they are?" Kat asked, staring.

Andy was trying to listen analytically. It sounded as if half the birds were saying "jeep" and the other half "crackle-crackle"; he wondered how they decided which ones said which. "How come they're all crowding back in one corner?" he asked.

"Heard us coming. They're better'n watchdogs, guineas are," Ellerton added with a touch of pride in his soft, rather toneless voice.

If all you want is noise and no brains, thought Andy as their approach made the whole flock turn like a school of black-and-white fish and flow into the opposite corner of the pen, long necks and tiny scarlet-trimmed heads outstretched. Decibels increased, if anything. Kat clapped her hands over her ears and hurried after Ellerton, who was heading for the nearest of the two sheds.

Andy followed, resolving to make a further study of guinea hens sometime. They might *all* be saying "jeep-crackle" but it would take time and close attention to be sure.

This half of the poultry house was reserved for laying hens and smelled richly of their feed in spite of the screened openings all down one side, but it was clean swept, airy, and well stocked with mash and water. Tiers of homemade wooden nests stuffed with fresh straw ran along one wall. "It's not your high-tech operation," Ellerton said placidly as they stood in the doorway. "But this here's the way hens like to live."

Certainly the few white-feathered matrons dozing on their straw beds appeared smugly content with their lot. A scattering of white pullets stalked here and there about the floor. They jostled one another and jerked alarmed glances toward the strangers, and after a moment Ellerton apologetically closed the door.

"The girls aren't used to visitors—only me," he explained. He gestured toward a small, mossy-roofed outbuilding farther down the path. "Le's go on to my office."

Inside, the weathered little building was neat and fresh painted, with big windows over a businesslike desk. "Fixed this place up myself from an old feed shed," Ellerton told them. "Funny kinda office, innit?" he added with a wink at Kat. "But it does fine for my funny kinda businesses."

"Eggs and poultry, and what else?" she asked.

"Bees—I got my wild clover honey for sale in some of them fancy ski-resort shops, Sugar Meadows and all. And then there's my graveyard job."

"Graveyard job?" Andy echoed.

"Old pioneer graveyard up yonder on the hill. I'm caretaker."

"Oh," said Kat. She seemed a little doubtful of her feelings about this job.

Andy was sure *he* wouldn't care for it. But he said only, "I didn't even know they still buried people in those real old places."

"Oh, it's not a *modren* cemetery. Old pioneers got it all to themselves. Harper's Mill Historical

Society, they're in charge of it. It's a real piece of history. But somebody got to keep the weeds down, and the stray dogs chased off. I was right here handy, so . . ." Ellerton smiled and rummaged in one of the drawers of the desk until he found a much-creased typewritten sheet. "Here y'are—now, you just show this list to your ma, and if you got any questions—"

"I've got one now," Kat told him. "Do white eggs really taste any different from brown eggs?"

Ellerton gave her his remarkable smile and shook his head. "No, but duck eggs—now, I'm partial to a duck-egg omelet, myself. I'll just give you half a dozen to try. You wanta see my duck pond? Come on—I got four, five different kindsa duck down there. . . ."

Half an hour later, laden with their sample of duck eggs and far more information about domestic fowl than they had known existed, the Petersons collected their other possessions from under the hazel bush and headed once more up the lane. As it tilted up and the view opened out over the valley, Kat stopped suddenly and pointed. "Hey, look."

It was a hay wagon, filled with kids and balloons, and pulled by Bonnie and Clyde, bumping along the far lower edge of the Buckles' hay field. Mr. Buckle was standing in the front of the wagon, behind a seated small figure—a girl. *She* was holding the reins. A faint jingling and rattling and laughing floated up to them as they watched.

"Now I wish we'd stuck around," Kat said forlornly. "I wish we had a little more free time. *I* want to learn to drive. Listen, we might just sit here and rest till they come back by, and then—"

"Kat—not today. We've got to get back to the Lodge with this stuff. *C'mon.*"

Impatiently, she turned her back on him and started on. "Well, I want to get to *know* some kids around here."

"Me too, but we don't belong at their birthday party until we do."

Kat flung him her quit-preaching look and jammed on her earphones. "Big, *immovable* Swede," she quoted under her breath.

Andy let it pass.

Following her up the steepest part of the lane, he glanced toward the woods; it was right about here he'd lost sight of the oddball kid.

And there was the same boy, standing right beside the big rock, waiting—as if he'd been there all along.

"Hey, there you are again!" said Andy—not very intelligently, he realized. "How come you ran away before?" he added.

"I didn't, really," replied the soft, raggedy little voice.

"Well—hid, then," Andy amended.

He got no response to that; the boy just looked at him. He was really a hard one to talk to.

Andy tried again. "You from somewhere around here?"

"Yes . . ." It sounded a little uncertain.

"Whereabouts d'you live?"

The boy hesitated, then said, "Around here."

Oh, well, Andy thought. "What's your name?" he asked.

"Jacob." Then, in that strangely urgent tone, the boy repeated, "*Somebody's got my bed.*"

Kat's voice came from a little way up the path. "I thought you were in such a hurry. . . . Who is it, that little kid again?"

Andy glanced at her and beckoned, then quickly turned back to Jacob. "Now stay put," he said, making a little patting gesture as if reassuring a stray dog. "My sister's harmless." To Kat, as she arrived at his side, he added, "I guess he's one of the neighbors."

She looked in silence at the hillside.

Andy did, too. Jacob was waiting obediently beside the rock. "Listen, about this bed," Andy began, when Kat broke in, sounding disgusted.

"Oh, *Andy*. What are you trying to pull?"

"What? I'm not trying to pull anything. All I did was ask him—"

"Save it. There's nobody *there*."

He turned to gape at her. "You going blind or something? The kid's standing right there, plain as day."

She threw him a withering look and started back up the hill. Bewildered, Andy swung back to the boy.

And there was nobody there.

CHAPTER THREE

Midsummer was the slack season at the Lodge. The typical groups that came, whether for one day or the weekend, were not vacationers but working groups, attending a seminar or a conference associated with their jobs, and in July and August they were scattered elsewhere on their holidays—or so Uncle Richard had explained to Dodie in that first phone call, adding easily that they really wouldn't have much to do but explore the trail walks around Hidden Creek and occasionally drive up to Sugar Meadows for a look at the view.

Well, maybe, in July and August. But it was still June, and twenty-two people were due to gather for a Writers' Workshop Thursday afternoon and stay (eating their heads off, if Mrs. Corey-who-cooks could be believed) until early Sunday. Two weeks before that, on the traumatic weekend when Uncle Richard and Todd had come to the parting of the ways, thirty librarians had been in residence.

"And I guess it was a wonder they got anything to eat at *all*, or their beds made up or *anything*," Kat told the others at supper Wednesday evening.

"What with all the rumpus and ruction and howdedo there was around here."

"Rumpus and ruction?" echoed Andy, fork arrested on its way to his mouth. "*Howdedo*?"

"Well, that's what Mrs. Corey called it," Kat told him shortly.

She was still being definitely short with him over his "imaginary" little kid on the hillside, whom she said he had invented just to bug her. He had protested in vain that he had invented nobody, nothing. "Would I have invented that *bed*?" he had demanded on the way home. "*Could* I have?"

Kat had refused to answer. But they both knew that imagination wasn't his sort of thing—it was Kat's. Ordinarily, he would be telling *her* she was just imagining something. It was confusing to both of them, having it all turned around.

Dodie said tolerantly, "Mrs. Corey has a fine repertoire of old-timey phrases. But I doubt if anything short of mayhem would've kept her from feeding those librarians—and probably making their beds, too, if everybody else had deserted. Thank heaven I've got her to see me through this weekend! Twenty-eight writers! *Quel cauchemar*! Kat, pass me the butter."

"Oh, I don't think it'll be an actual *nightmare*," remarked Andy. He, along with Kat, had picked up a rather peculiar smattering of French from living with Dodie, who loved emotional French catchwords. "Writers don't sound to me very wild and desperate, even twenty-eight of them."

"What if they've got twenty-eight artistic temperaments?" Kat put in darkly.

"I wouldn't mind *that*," said Dodie. "The nightmare is that I don't know any more about running a resort than I do about launching a space ship. I can't think how Richard managed."

"He didn't, very well," Andy reminded her.

Dodie took one of her rare detours into sentiment. "Poor old Rick! He trusted that *type* implicitly." She pronounced it the French way, "*teep*," which sounded wonderfully insulting.

"I wonder why he did?" Kat mused. "Mrs. Corey says she figured Todd had his hand in the till from the day he came. What's a 'till,' Dodie? The cash register?"

"The joint bank account too, in this case. Oh, Richard's a perfect *fool* about people and always has been," added Dodie, reverting to her more usual astringent self. "Andy, you want anything else to eat? Actually there isn't anything else, is there. Come on, kids, help me clear."

"I thought you said Mrs. Corey and Todd were in that egg scam together," Andy said to Kat as he constructed a perilous tower of plates and cups.

"I only said they might be. Because of Mr. Harper being her brother-in-law. Listen, let's ask Dodie now."

"Ask me what?" Dodie demanded from the sink. "Andy! Leave a plate or two for the next trip. In fact, leave. Kat, ask me what?"

"About getting our eggs from Mr. Buckle instead of that *yucky* Mr. Harper!"

Kat launched into a passionate description of Mr. Harper's utterly filthy poultry yard and his utterly rude behavior, and Ellerton's exemplary ones—"hen-friendly" was the triumphant term she used, adding, "Dodie, it's the kind of place hens *like* to live!" Andy, after depositing his leaning tower on the drainboard, went out the back door, confidently leaving the whole matter in her hands. It was not quite eight o'clock, and the day had been a beauty; even here in the woods there was plenty of light still, the clear lavender-blue light of summer evening. He crossed the ferny patch behind the cottage and headed down past the row of connected cabins forming The Annex to collect the grubbing hoe and shovel and rake he'd abandoned near the Lodge when Dodie's theatrical Gallic shriek, "*À moi!*" had called him to dinner.

Someone was coming toward him, up on the covered wooden walkway that ran along in front of the cabins from the main entrance of the Lodge. The housekeeper, it must be; she was unlocking the door of every room as she came, peering in briefly, relocking and going on, her footsteps brisk and hollow on the raised deck floor. Her husband was a carpenter—Dodie said he'd helped build the Lodge. What was their name? Not Corey. Not Harper.

"Hi, Mrs. Sweet," said Andy, taking a chance on a fairly sure thing. "Making sure everything's okay for those writers tomorrow, are you?"

"That's my job," she answered, stepping to the railing to squint down at him—and not correcting the name, so he must have guessed right. "Oh, it's the Peterson boy, isn't it? My glasses need changing, Martin's always saying so. Well, how are you liking us by now? The Lodge, I mean."

"I'll like it better when I get all that gunk—I mean salal—grubbed out from the west side. But the upper trail's looking pretty good. If those writers want to quit writing and take a walk, they can. Is that what writers do at a workshop? Write?"

"Not the ones we've had around here. They talk. Sounds like a roomful of parakeets in that dining room at lunchtime."

Andy made a mental note not to miss this phenomenon. As the housekeeper started for the next cabin, he had a thought. "Oh, Mrs. Sweet—you live around here, I s'pose?"

"Right down on the county road. First place toward town from the Buckles' lane. The Christmas tree farm."

"Oh! So that's what that is!" Andy had wondered about that stretch of young forest—all the trees so neatly spaced.

"That's what it is." Mrs. Sweet gave a little cackle of laughter. "Old Santa doesn't really bring 'em around on Christmas Eve, you know. Somebody's gotta grow 'em."

"Well—do you know a little kid who probably lives somewhere near you—maybe eight or nine years old—"

Mrs. Sweet was already shaking her head. "Nobody with kids lives near us. Between us and town there's only my brother-in-law Millard's place—he's an old widower—"

"I was thinking of the other direction."

"*Up* from the Buckles? Nobody," said Mrs. Sweet positively. "That's all just forest from there right on up to Sugar Meadows. Mostly gov'munt property. Why?"

"Oh . . . I just got to wondering," Andy said vaguely. "Well—g'night."

"Good night." Mrs. Sweet clumped on down the walkway and Andy wandered thoughtfully around to the west side of the Lodge where he had left the tool cart. Whichever farm that funny little Jacob kid came from, it plainly wasn't anywhere near the big rock where he liked to hang out. Next time I see him, Andy promised himself, I'll ask him again where he lives. And what his other name is. And about that *bed*. If he'll just stick around a couple of minutes and quit letting Kat scare him off. . . . Maybe I should go down that way alone sometime, Andy reflected as he restored the scattered tools to their built-in holders in the cart. Just slip off by myself . . .

But that seemed silly. Trundling the cart to its lockup under the broad Lodge deck, he asked himself exasperatedly how anybody could be scared of *Kat?*

The writers began arriving right after lunch next day, though they weren't really due until dinner.

"Oh, murder," Dodie said distractedly as she hung up the phone and abandoned her fresh-poured cup of coffee. "I'll have to go over to Reception right away." She pried off the old running shoes she wore when she didn't care what she looked like, and stepped into the pumps that always stood waiting, pigeon-toed, in the back hall. "Kat, the minute you're through eating get over to the laundry room and check on—"

"—the dinner napkins, and be back at four-thirty sharp to set tables. I already *know* what to do, Dodie, don't fuss and fidget."

"Fuss and fidget," Andy muttered into his ice cream. Kat was picking up a whole new Harper's

Mill vocabulary, while he battled vine maple roots in solitary exile. "Want me to carry bags or anything?" he asked hopefully.

But Dodie, peering into the speckled little mirror by the back door while she gave her mop of wiry, curly, auburn hair the little pushes and shoves and disciplinary yanks that mysteriously organized it into its usual shape, instructed him instead to tidy up the kitchen and put in another hour on the creek trail. "After that you and Kat can scamper down to the Buckles' and tell 'em we'll take their eggs. And if you're really longing to carry bags, show up at Reception—*clean*—at about four-thirty. You might be useful then. 'Bye, I'm gone."

The screen door gave its little opening shriek and the inconclusive sort of double-bounce it made when allowed to shut itself, invariably leaving a crack that invited flies. Andy got up and fastened it, then carried his plate and glass to the sink, grumbling to Kat that on the whole he'd never been so useful in his life as he'd been in the past week and a half. "I see you got your way about Mr. Leonard Harper," he added.

"Yep," Kat said with relish. She rose, finished her milk, thumped the glass down by her plate and headed for the back door.

"Hey, how about this tidying-the-kitchen bit?" Andy objected.

"She told *you* to. Meet you about two-thirty, and we'll go see Ellerton." The screen door shrieked again and bounced again.

"So long as I don't have to *scamper*," Andy growled as he went once more to eliminate the crack. But he was whistling as he began to rinse the dishes. Once he and Kat had discussed eggs with Ellerton, no reason they couldn't just drop in on Mr. Buckle, too—he'd said "any time"—and maybe discuss horses, and wagon rides, and driving.

By two-twenty he had cut back an encroaching rhododendron and hacked several yards of creeping blackberry from the creekside trail, which was going to be great if he ever got through with it. Ears still ringing from the constant noisy chattering of the creek rushing over its stones—he kept thinking of Mrs. Sweet's roomful of parakeets—he plodded back up to the cottage and into the shower. Ten minutes later he was plunging buoyantly down the steep shortcut beside Kat.

It was another fine day, sunny with little puff-ball clouds, and as they emerged from the woods and turned to follow the path past the weed-grown iron fence enclosing the little graveyard, they could hear blackbirds. Andy saw one, too, sitting right on a wrought-iron curlicue not ten feet away from them, whistling its liquid notes and shining blue-black in the sun.

"Look!" he exclaimed, pointing, and of course it flew, with the flash of scarlet he'd never really seen outside his bird book.

He did not see Jacob. He looked for him, as they passed the big rock near the edge of the woods, even hung back to peer into the shadows under the trees, but there wasn't a sign of him. Disappointed, a bit worried—though he told himself the kid must go home sometimes—he dawdled, in case his odd little friend might suddenly appear, grasshopper-like, after all. There was something about the boy, with his gravelly little voice and his missing bed, that tugged at him. He wondered guiltily if Jacob had decided he was no use at all at finding beds, and given up. Then he asked himself crossly why he should feel so *responsible*. Finally he caught up with Kat, who was in the middle of telling him a complicated story involving Mrs. Corey's sister's grandson's broken leg, and hadn't noticed he wasn't right behind her.

They rounded the screen of hazel bushes to start up the Buckles' drive and stopped in their tracks. The big hay wagon was drawn into the middle of the barnyard and the whole place swarmed with what looked like half the kids in the county. Andy's heart gave an acrobatic leap and began to pound.

"It's that 4-H group, it must be," Kat muttered, hastily beating a retreat. She was too late; Mr. Buckle had just appeared from the barn leading one of the giant horses. He spotted the twins and waved.

"Hi, Andy and Kat!"

This produced instant, total silence and focused every eye in the place on them.

Andy returned the "Hi," which came out sounding as if it needed sandpapering. He cleared his throat, sweeping a quick, eager glance over the watching faces—about a dozen, of varied ages. One or two looked friendly, most just curious, all wait-and-see cautious like the little kid in the woods. All, more than likely, named Harper or Corey or Sweet.

Well, we wanted to meet some of the kids around here, Andy told himself. So here they are; go meet 'em. "C'mon," he said to Kat, and started toward Mr. Buckle.

Mr. Buckle handed Clyde's lead strap to the nearest boy and came halfway, with a welcoming smile. "Just the day to use that rain check, if you want to join us."

Andy returned the smile with compound interest, and said, "Thanks! We'd really like that!"

"The only thing is," Kat said swiftly, "We're supposed to tell Ellerton it's okay about the eggs. I mean, first we'd better—"

"I'll tell 'im for you. Come on and let me introduce you around." He turned back to the group, slipping a reassuring big hand under Kat's elbow.

"Kids, this here's the Peterson twins. Andy and Kat, that's Edwin Harper there by the wagon wheel, and next to him Bill Harper—cousin, not brother—and Sue, she's Ed's sister, and Dawnelle Sweet, and Nick and Karl Corey, and—"

Andy lost track right away, of course. A few names stuck in his mind, attached to faces: Dawnelle Sweet because she had such black hair— blackbird black—and turquoise eyes like a Siamese cat's; Johnny Corey because he was the smallest, and freckled right down into his T-shirt neck and up under its chopped-off sleeves; Sam Clark because he grinned; and Evan Huddleston because his name wasn't Corey, Harper, or Sweet.

After a lot of mumbled "Glad t'meet yous" and "Me toos," punctuated by a few abrupt handshakes —the hands mostly smaller than Andy's but surprisingly strong—the worst bit was over. Andy stepped back with a relieved laugh, adding, "I s'pose we'll get you all straight some time or other."

He got no response beyond a couple of smiles and some awkward murmurs, but Mr. Buckle said easily, "Whole summer to do it in. Right now it's time t'hitch up. Sam, go bring that Bonnie out here. And Terry, you and Ed can fetch the harness." He turned to slap the massive sorrel rump beside him, said, "*Git* over there, Clyde," and the afternoon's routine was under way.

CHAPTER FOUR

For the next few minutes Andy, backed off to one side with Kat to be out from underfoot, watched hypnotized as the group of tongue-tied farm kids, now chattering Old Hands, transformed themselves into a smoothly functioning team. Bonnie was led from the barn to join Clyde in front of the high, slat-sided wagon. There they were both fitted with bridles, fed their hinged bits by a girl who could barely reach their mouths, and adorned with thick oval collars sprouting brass horns. Then a sort of sketchy network of dangling straps, jingling with rings and buckles, was thrown like a blanket over each broad back. Into or onto or through these basic items other straps were buckled or threaded or snapped—certain loops left loose and roomy, others cinched tight, none of it making much sense to Andy, who was staring, slack jawed, trying to follow the logic.

He became conscious that his mouth was open, and closed it, trying for a more nonchalant expression. He glanced at Kat as Mr. Buckle backed the horses into position on either side of the wagon tongue. She was standing unnaturally still and looking as remote as if she were all alone on the peak of Mount Everest. When he turned back to the hitching operation a couple of the 4-H'ers were just fastening the widest straps to the wagon by a few links of chain.

And all of a sudden it did make sense, the whole web of leather; he could see how the pull on one strap would be shared by another, how the main weight of the wagon would be taken by the collars resting against the horses' powerful shoulders and chests, and moved forward by the steel muscles of their hindquarters.

It was marvelous. He forgot about appearing nonchalant and cried, *"Wow!"* with unrestrained enthusiasm, bringing his palms together in a ring- ing slap.

All the heads swiveled toward him. Kat said, *"Andy!"* in a scandalized whisper, and Mr. Buckle turned with a smile and questioning eyebrows.

"I see how it works," Andy explained, feeling a rush of heat to his ears and neck, but too enthralled with his private discovery of the principles of en- gineering and team hitching to care if he was bright red or not.

"Ve-ry good, Andy!" Mr. Buckle commented. "Okay, you 4-H'ers, let's see if you can name *all* the parts today."

Standing alongside Bonnie, he pointed abruptly at the widest strap—the one that stretched directly from her collar to the wagon.

"Trace!" yelled the group.

His finger moved swiftly to a curlicued brass ring on the highest point of her rump, the center of an octopus of straps.

"Trace carrier!" yelled the voices.

The finger moved on to this strap and that buckle and the other bolt snap, and the voices kept with it, sometimes raggedly as in "layer on breeching seat," more often in triumphant unison as in "ring bit!" "throat latch!" "hame!"

It was quite a performance.

When it was over, Mr. Buckle said, "Good job! All aboard!" and there was a general surge toward the wagon. But amid the scrambling and elbowing, not one person, Andy noted, failed to snatch a quick glance at him and Kat—obviously to see how they were taking it. How impressed they were.

Okay, I'm impressed! Andy retorted silently. No need to act so smug, though—what you can learn, I can too. And *will*.

Kat was still on her mountaintop, her profile in neutral, her emotions a secret—or possibly just on hold. For her a lot would depend, Andy knew, on how the wagon ride turned out, and what she could salvage from it in the way of beginner's luck or aptitude. Kat had to show up well in *something*, right away. After that she opened up warmly and freely, and didn't mind being taught more. Andy didn't care how clumsy he looked, first or last, so long as he learned what he wanted. And he wanted to learn this—about as much as he had ever wanted anything.

They scrambled up into the wagon with everybody else, and stood close together just over the left rear wheel, beyond which the ground seemed surprisingly far away. The others, too, were ranged around the slatted sides, elbows hooked over the top rail, except the tallest and skinniest of the boys, Sam Clark, who climbed to the highest seat just behind the horses. It was evidently his turn to start the driving. He sat down with a flourish behind Clyde, took the reins from Mr. Buckle, who was standing just behind his left shoulder, and yelled, "Everybody set?"

"Let 'er go," said Mr. Buckle.

Sam flapped the reins, said, "*Hup!*" and the wagon lurched into motion.

For the first few seconds Andy was too startled to do anything but grab for the rail and brace his feet; Kat staggered wildly, clutched a slat and him, too. He felt as if he had somehow stepped into a cement mixer instead of a farm wagon; the bouncing and banging and rattling and grinding noises were all just the same. He hung on, shouting with surprised laughter; it was hard to believe the wheels underneath were round, not square.

"Never rode in a thing without springs before," he yelled to the boy standing next to him—little freckled Johnny Corey, as it happened.

"Gets smoother up ahead a ways," Johnny yelled back.

But first it got rougher, as the horses turned across the deep ruts of the driveway entrance to head uphill. The passengers lurched back and forth; the whole wagon tilted and jounced and rocked, seemed certain to go right over. Then they were onto the gravel and the horizon steadied, and there they were, rolling along up the lane toward the cemetery, noisy as ever but on an even keel.

"Wow! This is great!" cried Andy. He leaned down to shout in Kat's ear. "You like it?"

He could see her lips move, but whatever she said was inaudible. Her eyes were wide, and her profile strained and white. Obviously she did not exactly *like* it yet.

She will, he told himself optimistically, and peered over her head to see where they could be going; certainly not up the little cow path.

But where the graveled lane ended, multiple shallow ruts curved away to the right, tracing a grassy track along in front of the cemetery to its

entrance gates, which were wrought iron like the
fence, and stood open. It looked as if cars had
parked in that patch of flattened weeds opposite.
People must come to look at the old graves, Andy
thought as the wagon rattled by. Maybe find their
great-great-grandma's name on a stone. Kat and I
ought to look around in there sometime—might
see some real old dates.

They would not, of course, see any names they
knew (aside from Harper, Corey and Sweet).
Dodie's forebears had all died in places like Akron
or Chicago, and the Petersons, presumably, in
Sweden. Briefly, Andy remembered the bearded
giant boarding the bus, and wondered if Sweden
was where his unknown father had been off to,
that long ago day. Dodie had never said. She'd
said remarkably little, ever, about their father,
merely giving terse answers to direct questions.

What was he like?

Very handsome, very intelligent, very stubborn.

Why did he go away?

*He found he did not care for family life—or the
United States.*

But didn't he love us?

*He loved himself better. I gave you priority. We
agreed to disagree.*

That was about all he and Kat knew about their
other parent. But when one thought it over, it was

quite enough. If he'd been able to *choose* his father,
Andy thought now as he watched Mr. Buckle, he'd
have picked one who could handle horses.

The wagon lurched as it turned again, at the
lower end of the cemetery, and started back toward
the house across the top of the hay field. Sam gave
a snap to the reins and the horses surged into a
brisk trot, harness jingling like sleigh bells. Andy's
mind cleared of everything but the huge, bright
day, the moving air and puffball clouds, the sun
warm and the harness ringing, kids shouting at
each other, and the broad sorrel rumps ahead bobbing up and down. At the far edge of the field Sam
changed places with one of the girls, who turned
the horses downhill along the fence line. Going
downhill at a trot over rough ground was exhilarat-
ing—too much so, for Kat; in the midst of one
quite spectacular bump Andy noticed that she was
entirely airborne, both feet off the wagon's wooden
floor. His own feet felt as if they were resting on
a carpet of vibrating ballbearings instead of planks.
He put a hand on her shoulder to provide a little
ballast, and she gave him a quick, scared glance
and didn't shrug it off. As for him, he was getting
used to it, bouncing like a dried pea in a pan, and
no longer convinced the wagon was bound to over-
turn. The other kids were showing off what vet-
erans they were, each scrambling forward to take
the reins in turn. And finally Mr. Buckle sum-

moned Andy, adding cheerfully, "Kat, you come on up front too. You're next."

With an inner thump of excitement Andy made his way forward and climbed over the slats to the high perch above and behind Clyde, feeling like an extra-large canary venturing out of its safe cage onto a limb. From this angle Clyde was foreshortened into a vast coppery pear shape, his broad rounded hindquarters tapering forward to his flaxen mane and two pricked ears. Bonnie, nodding her head impatiently down there on the left, looked more like the usual sort of horse.

Mr. Buckle was leaning over Andy, threading the reins into his hands just so, the thick straps between the middle knuckles of the first two fingers, thumbs free, palms close together. "Keep both reins pulled back so's to keep the horses even, and their heads up," he was saying. "Try to feel their mouths—but gentle-like. Use your wrists, see? You talk through your hands to horses. To start movin', give 'em a little slap with the reins and a '*hup.*' Pull on the right rein to turn thataway, pull on the left for the other. Pull both and yell 'ho' if you wanta stop. If you wanta trot, lift the reins up higher off their back and give 'em another little '*hup.*' That's their signal. And just relax. They know a lot more about this than you do—they won't let you get in trouble."

Andy threw a grin at him over his shoulder, took

a deep breath and clamped his knuckles on the reins, which were at once heavier and more supple than he had expected, gave them a brisk snap and said "*Hup!*" The vast obedient creatures ahead of him strained forward instantly, and the wagon followed. And there he was, driving 4,450 pounds of horse across the top of the field.

He was far too excited to sort out the stream of sensations, discoveries, surprises and impressions that fled through him in the next few minutes like a speeded-up movie reel. They changed too fast and he was too busy trying to keep the reins taut and his wrists level and the horses' heads up to take note of anything else. His chief impulse, difficult to control, was to yell and whoop; his biggest surprise was that the reins seemed made of rubber, giving him no information about how hard a pull was too hard and what was "gentle-like." His overriding discovery, impossible to ignore, was that his hands were aching with fatigue—almost, it seemed, before he'd started. But the fact was he'd driven the width of the field, made the turn up toward the cemetery and was now proceeding— at a venturesome trot—along the grassy track past the wrought-iron gates. Mr. Buckle's voice sounded in his ear just as he was wondering how much longer he could keep his knuckles clenched on those thick straps.

"Just turn 'em into the lane there and pull up,"

came the welcome instructions. "That's it, good enough. I think you got a knack for this, son. C'mon now, Kat, you can take 'em home."

Relinquishing the reins with stiff fingers, Andy shot a quick diagnostic glance at his twin as she climbed past him into the high seat, neck rigid, face expressionless, exactly as if she were climbing into the dentist's chair. Scared spitless, he decided, and not going to show it. He jumped down into the box of the wagon, flexing his hands. If *his* were tired, after all his daily root-grubbing . . . Well, no use worrying. If he knew Kat, she was going to drive that team same as these other kids, and neither storm nor sleet nor a cageful of tigers would stop her.

She slapped the reins and was off to a smooth start, looking about as big as a good-sized mosquito perched up there above Clyde with her hands stiffly correct, her back so straight it bowed in a little. Andy relaxed. Mr. Buckle had saved the easiest bit for her, he realized—a bare hundred yards down a graveled, level lane. Three minutes and she'd be home free.

He had forgotten about the rutted turn into the barnyard. So had she, apparently, because she raised her hands to signal a trot just before they got there—going to whirl in with a flourish, show 'em all; Andy could read her mind. Instead she came within an inch of bouncing right off her perch and down into the road—Mr. Buckle grabbed her or she would have. He grabbed the reins, too, because her hands had flown up, along with her auburn braid and the rest of her; Andy, standing directly behind, could see right underneath her for a second.

Behind *him*, not quite masked by the wagon's rattling, he heard one giggle, quickly suppressed. His first impulse was to whirl and glare; he nearly dislocated his neck resisting it. Ignore 'em—that was the thing to do.

A moment later the wagon was safely into the barnyard, Mr. Buckle driving with one hand, the other arm still around Kat, who kept making instinctive little grabs at the reins and checking them, fragments of apology tumbling out of her in a high, mortified voice.

"Now, then, no harm done a-tall," Mr. Buckle was assuring her. "Those ol' ruts are bad—I oughta hitch Clyde to the drag and smooth 'em out. I keep meanin' to. *Ho*, Bonnie, this'll do right here." Pulling up in front of the first barn, he knotted the reins around the whipstand and made the big half step, half jump to the ground, turning to lift Kat down beside him.

Andy leaped down too, just as she was saying, "We have to go now." She grabbed his arm and tried to tug him toward the lane.

He didn't move, and trapped her hand against

his ribs so she couldn't, either. "We sure appreciate you letting us come along!" he told Mr. Buckle. "And letting us drive—that was great! We prob'ly both made a lot of mistakes," he added cheerfully.

"You both did fine for your first-time try," insisted Mr. Buckle. "Don't you want to stick around for some lemonade and a little hitching practice?"

"Well . . . I guess we better get back," Andy answered, conscious of Kat's fingers digging into his arm like claws. Directing an all-purpose wave toward the 4-H'ers swarming down from the wagon, he called a couple of "so longs," got a couple of "see ya's" in reply, then walked unhurriedly out of the barnyard, Kat at his side.

The instant they were beyond the concealing hazel thicket, Kat jerked free of him and broke into a run. Fifty feet ahead she halted to yank a tissue out of her pocket and blow her nose infuriatedly, then stalked on. Sighing, Andy lengthened his stride to catch up. Now he had a problem—Kat— just when he wanted nothing more than to gloat about driving. So she'd made one goof, and she had to be perfect. Why was it all *his* fault somehow or other?

"Doesn't do any good to be mad at *me*," he told her reasonably as he came abreast. "Wouldn't have done any good back there to run like a scared rabbit, either."

"I'm *not* a scared rabbit. But I don't like this

place! I wish we'd never come to Hidden Creek! I wish I was already at music camp! I hate horses."

Her eyes were filling and her face was bright pink under the scattered freckles. That giggle must have really hurt. Instantly Andy was on her side. Never mind if she was thin-skinned and a lot too hard on herself. She couldn't help it.

"Okay, listen, I wanta learn to drive, but you don't need to have anything more to do with horses. You like Mr. Buckle, don't you? You can just go see him sometimes when we get the eggs. . . . In fact, *I'll* get the eggs. You don't even need to—"

"No." Kat flipped her braid back over her shoulder, swallowed hard and began to regain her natural color as they trudged on up the slope. "We'll both go. And we'll both drive. I'll get used to the horses. It's just—they're so *big*. But I'm gonna learn to drive them. I *am*. If that real small boy with all the freckles can do it . . . he's smaller than me, even—"

She went on talking herself around, but Andy suddenly quit listening. They had reached the place near the big rock and as he glanced up toward it, he saw Jacob standing there, patient.

Kat walked on, still explaining. Andy hissed at her, then halted. "Hey, Jacob. Hi."

As always, Jacob said, "Hiyuh."

"Listen, Jacob," Andy said firmly. Three things

he was going to ask this time, and he meant to get all three said. "Whereabouts d'you live, anyhow? And what's your other name, your last name? And what about this *bed?*"

Jacob shifted his weight and looked a little troubled, but didn't say anything.

Maybe I went too fast, thought Andy. "Jacob?" he said tentatively.

"Yeah?"

"What's your other name? Your family name?"

"Sweet. I'm Jacob Sweet."

"Oh. That figures. So whereabouts d'you live? Toward town, or—"

Jacob interrupted him, in that special, compelling tone. "Somebody's got my bed."

Andy took a deep breath, resolved this time to get to the bottom of that, at least. "Yeah, you told me. But what d'you *mean?* Your brother take it over, or something?"

"I don't have any brother."

"Then somebody took it away?"

Kat was stalking back down the path. "Hey, I was *talking* to you. Why d'you keep getting lost when I'm—" Andy flapped a hand at her and she stopped short, then began edging closer.

"So who's got it, then?" Andy asked Jacob. No answer. "Don't you know?" he added in some exasperation.

Jacob gave a slight shake of his head.

It was like talking to a riddle. Andy thought a minute. Kat was nearly at his elbow now, demanding, "Where is he?"

"Right up there," Andy told her, nobly refraining from adding, *exactly where I told you before.* To Jacob he said, "You mean somebody stole it."

"Yes. Somebody stole it."

"Out of your house?"

Oddly, this seemed to disconcert Jacob, who apparently didn't know how to answer. Under his breath Andy muttered to Kat, "There's something funny about this kid."

There was an instant's silence, which Kat shattered. "Yes, there is," she retorted loudly. *"Very funny. Ha ha ha."* He swung around to stare at her, and found her again pink with anger, her eyes bright with tears. "And the funniest thing about him is he isn't *there.* And *you're* not the least bit funny, Andy Peterson, so just knock it off, okay?"

"Wait a minute!" Andy was as shocked as if she'd hit him across the face. This couldn't be happening—not again. "Kat! You *know* I wouldn't—"

"I know you *are.* I never thought you'd be so *mean.* Right when I was feeling bad anyway, and you have to go and make dumb *jokes*—"

"I'm not joking!" Andy glanced toward Jacob to make sure he was still right there in plain sight. Then he grabbed Kat's arms and pulled her around in front of him, to face the rock.

"*Look,*" he commanded. "See for yourself, if you don't believe me. There he *is*."

Kat craned about to give him a startled glance over her shoulder, then went very still, staring at the hillside—first toward the rock and then all around it, though Jacob had not moved. After a long moment, she whispered in a small, bewildered voice, "But I don't see anybody."

"Now who's making jokes," Andy said indignantly.

"But I don't! I really don't."

"You *must,*" Andy protested. "By the rock." He pointed past her cheek, and watched her sighting down his finger. Slowly she shook her head. "But you're looking right at him!" Baffled, Andy checked Jacob again himself, adding, "And he's looking straight at you."

"Andy," Kat said shakily. She pulled out of his grasp and turned to search his face with wide, uneasy eyes. "Andy—do you feel okay?" she asked him.

And she definitely wasn't joking now.

CHAPTER FIVE

B y four-thirty, when he walked over to the Lodge to show up, *clean*, as Dodie had ordered, Andy was in an unaccustomed and extremely uncomfortable state of mind. Instead of tranquilly looking forward to sizing up the writers while carting their bags around, he was worrying—about himself, and Kat, and what he was beginning to think of as the latest Jacob-sighting.

He had certainly sighted Jacob. He had seen him, heard him, spoken to him. But Kat had seen nobody. Andy believed her now.

She believed him now, too. That is, she still didn't believe in Jacob, but she believed . . . the fact was, she believed Andy was seeing things. Well, he was. He was seeing a little towheaded kid who kept saying somebody'd got his bed. Why should I have made that up? Andy asked himself exasperatedly. How *could* I? I'd never have thought of it in a million years.

This afternoon, as usual, when he had turned back to look once more, Jacob was gone. But this time Andy had gone after him; he'd scrambled up the bank beside the path and through the fringe of weeds and blackberry, regardless of scratches, right over to the trees and the big rock, determined to get his hands on Jacob, shake some answers out of him. The rock was farther from the path than he'd realized, and bigger, much bigger—a boulder the size of a van thrusting straight out of the ground, probably a chunk of the underlying granite showing through the soil. Standing right beside it, he'd thought it looked like some kind of huge crouched animal, a mammoth dog or something, just raising its head from sleep.

There was nobody else there beside it—nobody behind it or anywhere around it. There weren't any footprints, either, though those might not show in such a mixture of weeds and salal and fir needles. There was no sign at all that Jacob had ever stood there.

Andy had plodded slowly back to the path— a little more careful of briars this time—and slid down the bank to where Kat waited.

"Maybe it was a ghost," she'd whispered, her eyes enormous.

He'd only growled, "Don't be silly," and started home.

And ever since, he'd been alternately fuming and puzzling about it, his peace of mind broken up and scattered like the contents of a dumped-out drawer. *Was* he just "seeing things"? That would be a first for him. Kat, he kept telling himself irritably, was the one with the overactive imagination; he'd always been the literal, practical type. So was Jacob real or unreal? If unreal, what kind of unreal? A spook? A Munchkin? A little man from Mars?

His mind recoiled from the very question. What he could see with his own eyes was *real*. If only I could touch him once, he thought, that would prove it. . . . Very funny, he'd never let me get close enough. But I'll prove it anyway.

Think of some evidence, he commanded himself. Stuff you did see with your own eyes—and couldn't have made up.

All right. He'd seen a little kid, no older than nine or ten, not as tall at Kat. Kind of skinny. Towheaded. Gravelly, earnest little voice. Wearing . . . well, he could never remember exactly what Jacob was wearing. Just—clothes. That was the *trouble* with Jacob, Andy thought irritably. *One* trouble. You got talking to him and forgot to notice things, forgot questions you meant to ask. Even his features were hard to remember—except that his usual expression was wary and patient. A funny mixture. And . . . tired. Andy remembered this bit with a strange little twist of his insides. Jacob always looked frail and tired.

So why should that bother him? So the kid was tired. With no bed, he probably hadn't been getting enough sleep.

Andy shook himself like a wet dog, trying to throw off his thoughts, which seemed to him to be getting remarkably silly. Flinging open the main door of the Lodge with unnecessary vehemence, he presented himself to Dodie. She greeted him with relief, informed him in a melodramatic mutter that she was having a *crise de nerfs*, and told him to get busy sorting people into room numbers and carrying their bags.

He spent the next couple of hours making himself useful. It passed the time, it was better than grubbing out salal, and he made a number of observations concerning writers that usually he would have found intensely interesting. But his heart wasn't in it. At dinner he was silent. (This went unnoticed because Dodie wasn't.) At bedtime he was still disgruntled, frustrated, and painfully disturbed. What *was* this, anyhow? Was *he* having a *crise de nerfs*? Usually he wasn't even aware of having *nerfs*.

At breakfast Kat's slightly strained efforts to act perfectly normal nearly provoked him into bugging out his eyes at her and waggling his fingers in his ears. During his solitary morning, grubbing out red huckleberry volunteers (full of the tiny sour fruit, on which he browsed as he worked) and listening to the creek's unending clamor, he felt increasingly the need to consult somebody else— some grown-up. But who? Not Dodie, because

. . . well, he didn't know quite why, he just knew he couldn't risk it. Not Mr. Buckle, either—not now. In fact he was glad he'd kept forgetting to ask if Mr. Buckle knew that boy. He'd probably be like Kat, and think Andy was crazy. Andy couldn't really visualize trying to explain. When you came right down to it, it was impossible to explain to *anybody*.

About eleven o'clock, when he knew Kat would be setting the lunch tables and Dodie busy in the office, Andy threw down his grubbing hoe, left the cart beside the creek and plunged down the short-cut to the path and the big rock, determined to have it out with the source of the problem, Jacob himself.

And of course, now that he wanted him, Jacob was nowhere to be seen.

For a while Andy hung around on the path, peering into the fringes of the woods, staring at every shadow, every weed clump in the clearing around the big crouching rock. He tried calling—feeling like a half-wit, embarrassed at the sound of his own voice. Insects hummed, a blackbird whistled, the sun climbed toward noon, and the clearing with its enigmatic rock remained empty. Nobody answered.

With a last resentful glare Andy turned away and wandered irresolutely a few steps down the path, unable to go back to his grubbing hoe without *some* answer from *somebody*. Another blackbird called, this time from the direction of the cemetery, and he glanced back toward it—and thought of Ellerton.

Ellerton and his funny jobs . . . Yesterday from the wagon he'd noticed the cluster of beehives, looking like tiny rickety apartment houses, in the pasture just down beyond the graveyard's iron fence. What with the bees and the grave tending, Ellerton must go up and down this little cow path pretty often.

Andy turned and strode swiftly down the lane, past the Buckles' turn-in with only a quick glance into the quiet barnyard, and on downhill until he was even with the long, low roofs of the poultry sheds. There he pushed through the lane-side tangle of hazel and weeds into the sloping, oak-studded glade beyond. With a wary eye out for poison oak, which was rampant here, he made for the stand of maple he'd noticed at one end of the duck pond. From there Ellerton's little kingdom was all in plain sight.

To his satisfaction, Ellerton, too, was in plain sight, perched on a stump like some odd, bony species of bird himself, hugging his knees and watching a white duck zigzag about the pond, quacking fussily, and trailed by a line of small, squeaking puffball editions of herself, each with its little arrow-shaped wake. He saw Andy at once, unfolded himself and waved a greeting.

"Late brood. Fust time they been on the water," he said with a nod toward the string of ducklings. "Doin' fine, aren't they?"

"Yeah, great." Andy picked his way around the brushy end of the pond to a neighboring stump seat and joined him. "Just taking a breather from working on Uncle Richard's nature trails," he explained hastily, in case Ellerton should think it odd of him to come—then immediately realized it might seem odder still to walk half a mile for a breather. Now that he *was* here, he couldn't imagine how to lead up to his question.

But Ellerton helped him. "Hear you tried your hand at drivin' those Belgians yestiddy," he remarked in his toneless, placid voice, "Kids all love Harry's Belgians."

"Oh—uh—speaking of kids," Andy plunged in, grabbing his chance. "I was just wondering—I guess this is kind of a funny question, but—" He broke off. *Why* did the question all at once seem so funny-peculiar, and so hard to ask? Ellerton was waiting with a slight frown, watching his lips attentively. "Well—I just wondered—did you ever happen to see a little kid, a boy, sort of hanging around up near the woods at the top end of the lane? When you were going up to tend the bees or something?"

Polite but puzzled, as well he might be, Ellerton said, "I don't gener'ly *go* very near the woods."

"Well, I mean—you know that great big rock? Right around that clearing."

"Oh, Beaver Rock. I do pass there. . . . Oh, I guess I've seen boys now and then—can't say I ever noticed anybody specially. Kids don't seem to play up there much. Probably a lotta poison oak, like there is around the pond here. Anyway, they're usually down here, clusterin' around the horses." Ellerton smiled his warming smile and turned to watch the ducklings again, and Andy dropped the subject with relief. Ellerton might have seen Jacob and he might not—but he had never spoken with him. He could've failed to hear Jacob's usual soft "Hiyuh." In any case it was just too tricky a subject to pursue.

A few minutes later he escaped and plodded back back up the lane, bored with himself for wasting energy on a fool's errand. He spared a resentful glance for the rock as he came even—and there was Jacob, looking as if he were expecting Andy, as if he'd been waiting uncomplaining for hours. And he was definitely *right there*, plain as day, real as anybody, though a little farther away from the path than before. Plainly he wasn't about to let himself be touched. Well, there was no need to touch him, or to prove anything to anybody, either.

"So *there* you are. Now, listen," Andy said without preliminaries. "You just listen, okay? What you mean is, you want me to do something about your bed, is that it?"

"Yes," Jacob said earnestly.

"*What*, then? What d'you want me to do?"

"Get it back for me," said Jacob in his ragged, patient little voice. "I don't have any place to sleep."

Andy opened his mouth, hesitated, and closed it, his irritation dissolving. You just couldn't stay mad at Jacob. Besides, asking ordinary logical questions—where do you live, who are you, why do you keep hiding, who's got the bed—wasn't the way to go at this. Jacob evaded or simply didn't answer. Think of something else, Andy commanded himself.

Finally he said, "Okay, now look. If I try to get it for you, will you do something for me?"

"I will if I can."

Andy took a long breath. "Then quit playing hide-and-seek with my sister. Stick around long enough next time for her to see you!"

"She can see me any time she wants to," Jacob said. "She doesn't really look."

"But—but—but she *did*. Yesterday, anyway. Maybe before that—" Andy thought back. Both other times, when he'd sighted Jacob, Kat had been listening to a tape, which always made her deaf, dumb, and blind, as he well knew. And the second time, she'd been mad at him besides, and concentrating on that. . . . "Well, yeah. Sometimes she's thinking about something else, but yesterday she was staring right *at* you! At least I . . . thought so." But I was wrong, I must have been, he told himself, and anyway she was mad at me then, too. . . .

Jacob shifted his feet and glanced away uncomfortably. "Lots of people don't really look at things," he said. "You do, though."

And *that* was no answer—if anything, it was part of the problem. Andy clawed a hand through his forelock. This was like trying to pin down an eel. "Well, can't you help any?" he persisted. "You said you'd try—if I'd help you. So come on. What do I tell her to do?"

Jacob sighed, as though he would explain further if he knew how. Finally he repeated, "She has to really look." He frowned down along the path, and added hurriedly, "I have to go now."

"No, wait," Andy protested, darting a quick glance to see who was coming. The path was empty. And of course, when he turned back, Jacob was gone.

The oldest trick in the book, he thought, disgusted with himself. How does he do that, anyway, drop through a trapdoor? Without bothering to climb up through the brambles again to look, he started back to the Lodge. There wasn't any trap-door up there by the rock, and he knew it. What he still didn't know—anyway couldn't prove—was whether that little kid was a kid, or a hallucination, or indigestion. Or what to do to make Kat see him, too.

CHAPTER SIX

The writers' lunch was scheduled for 12:30. Andy waited till 12:35 before trundling his tool cart over to the Lodge to its lockup—mainly because he wanted to hear that roomful of parakeets, also because Kat would be coming off her pre-lunch duties about then. The parakeets didn't disappoint him; he could hear them from clear outdoors as he unlocked the toolshed under the deck. And Kat emerged from the kitchen door just as he reached it.

"Move, I want out of here," she said unceremoniously, pushing him aside. "Phwooh! *Quel brou-haha* in that kitchen!"

Andy interpreted this easily. "Dodie still having her *crise de nerfs?*"

"She's waiting tables—that extra waiter didn't show up. Mrs. Corey-who-cooks is having the *crise de nerfs*, because the extra waiter is her son— and is *he* ever going to get chewed out!" Kat flapped the problem away with both hands. "What're you doing over here?"

"Came to catch you alone. I thought Dodie'd be at the cottage. What's for lunch?"

Kat glanced at him suspiciously. "Why'd you want to catch me alone?"

"Lunch, Kat. I asked first."

"Peanut butter or cheese. No snails on toast. There's some homemade doughnuts—Mrs. Buckle's special. I—I walked down to the Buckles' by myself, Andy, a while ago. About ten o'clock."

Andy absorbed this news without comment, but with an increasing sensation of everything being out of joint. Both of them all of a sudden having private errands down that hill.

Kat hurried on, "I talked to Mr. Buckle. About something. I—"

"You don't have to tell me anything you don't want to," Andy said stolidly.

"I asked him if he'd give me some driving lessons," Kat blurted. "Alone. With nobody there to watch—and giggle."

Andy stopped walking and stared at her. "What'd he say?"

"He said he would! And you needn't tell me it'd cost too much because he never charges kids anything! He said so. He said he'd *like* to teach me."

"Just you?" Andy asked after a minute. "Not me too?"

"*You* seemed to be doing just fine on your own." There was a leftover of yesterday's resentment still in Kat's voice. "I didn't think you'd want any lessons."

"Well, I *would've*. So you're all wrong there."
Andy thought he might not be able to stand it if
she was the one who got lessons, when she didn't
want them half as bad as he did.

"Okay, then," Kat said quickly. Her face and
voice both cleared. "We can take them together.
He even asked if you wanted to come, too."

Well. That was more like it; the out-of-joint
world began to right itself, and take on its usual
upbeat form. "So when do we start?"

"Tomorrow, maybe when we go down to get
more eggs." Kat started walking again, talking
busily. "Mrs. Corey used up every one of old
Leonard Harper's, making angel food cakes and
custards, and she'll need more for Sunday breakfast."

"We could get those today. I want—to go down
the hill again anyhow—and this time take you
along."

Kat looked at him. "This time?"

"I went down alone this morning too. To find
Jacob." It wasn't necessary, Andy decided, to mention *not* finding him at first—or questioning Ellerton.

Kat's expression grew as still as Jacob's itself.
She half turned her head away without taking her
eyes from Andy; they seemed darker, without the
little green and gold lights they usually had, which
meant she was seriously worried. And she wasn't

the only one, thought Andy. He said nothing more, having as yet no idea how to explain to her that she had to *really look*—and she asked no questions at all, which was unheard of, for Kat. They were both beginning to behave as they never had in their lives—holding back from discussing something, feeling *apart* somehow.

This has got to stop, Andy told himself in a kind of angry fright. It's turning us into two other people.

The silence drew out. They walked across the clearing past the long annex with its raised deck, both looking elsewhere now, like a couple of strangers, Kat absently doing left-handed scales against her shirt front. Mrs. Sweet, the housekeeper, came out of the next-to-last door in the row, which was open; Andy could hear a vacuum whining away inside. Her two chambermaids must still be finishing up the rooms; pretty late for that. She looked cross as she thumped down the wooden steps at the end of the deck.

"Anything the matter?" Andy asked as they passed her.

"Oh, it's that Becky—my niece—she's Fay's extra this weekend and you'd think she never made a bed in her life. You can bet I'll have a thing or two to say to her ma! Sixteen years old and still can't clean a washbowl right. I tell *you*—"

Still grumbling, she headed for the parking lot and her midday break, presumably to join her own family's belated lunch—and Andy bet it wasn't just cheese or peanut butter. *Her* children were probably capable of cooking whole banquets as well as cleaning washbowls properly. He wondered who her children were—and suddenly thought he knew.

"Hey, I bet she's Dawnelle's mother," he said to Kat as they reached the back door of the cottage.

"What?" Kat sounded preoccupied. "Who's Dawnelle?"

"You remember. That girl with the Siamese cat eyes and the real black hair—one of the 4-H'ers. Mrs. Sweet's eyes look just like that, don't you think so?"

"*I* don't know," Kat said impatiently. "Were they blue? I don't exactly remember which was Dawnelle. There were so *many* of those kids. I didn't get any of them straight."

Andy's attention suddenly focused. "You remembered that Johnny—the little freckly one," he reminded her.

"Yes, well, because he was smaller than *me*—and *driving*. I'm going to learn, you know that, Andy? I'm *going* to." She flung open the screen and headed for the bread box. "Only not with all those kids looking at me. That was *awful*. I just felt like

. . . That's why I want some private lessons. So I can sort of catch up, and—you want chunk peanut butter or smooth?"

"Grilled cheese," said Andy. Automatically he fastened the screen door and went to get the cheese from the refrigerator, but he was no longer thinking about food. He was realizing that Jacob might have caught on to something after all. Something he himself had never noticed, well as he knew Kat.

Absently he began to build himself a sandwich, thinking hard. In a moment he said, "What color are Dodie's eyes?"

"Dodie's *eyes*?" Kat repeated blankly. She turned; he could feel her examining him. "Brown," she said. "Brown*ish*. Like mine."

"Yeah," he said, relieved. "What color are those running shoes she wears around in the mornings? No fair looking," he added, edging between Kat and the back entry.

"Andy? Running shoes? Have you lost your—"

"It's just a little—sort of test. I'm trying to find out something. Just tell me the color."

"How do *I* know? Let's see. Blue, aren't they? With those long white commas on the sides. Or else white with blue commas."

"Those were the old ones." Andy stepped aside. The current ones, waiting in the entry in abandoned attitudes to be replaced by the equally familiar brown pumps, were gray with dark blue commas.

"Well, I forgot she got new ones. They're all practically alike anyhow, and what *difference* does it make what color Dodie's shoes are?"

"Not any," Andy mumbled. That was a dumb test anyhow. He wished he could think of some better ones. But it might be Kat *didn't* really look. At least at things she didn't have any special feelings or thoughts about. Then what *was* she looking at all the time? What did she think about— besides music? If he knew her so well, why didn't he know that?

"Are you going to grill that sandwich, or just stand there forever holding the skillet?" Kat asked, elbowing him aside to get a knife from the drawer.

He came to and began to cook his lunch, but he was still trying to find answers to those apparently easy questions. Obviously he *didn't* know Kat very well, though they'd been living almost identical lives, side by side, since he was fifteen minutes old. Of course they were anything but identical; they knew that; everybody knew it. But in another way they were so close that trying to see inside her mind was like trying to see inside his own. He lacked practice at that, usually being more interested in somebody else. Kat was always doing it— peering into herself and apparently fascinated by the view, issuing little bulletins about how she *felt* about everything, and trying to find out why she felt it.

Well, that was one thing she kept looking at— herself. But she sometimes looked as hard inside other people. *He* liked to just relax and watch them, like a movie. But she knew a Possible Friend from a Don't Bother long before he'd got past the shape of their ears or the way they smiled. And once her attention was really caught, she zeroed in on them the way she practiced Bach—the way a heron finds fish. She was probably X-raying *him* right now.

"Andy, your sandwich is burning! Can't you smell?"

He yanked the skillet off the burner and scooped out his sandwich, wondering if his one laborious little answer had anything to do with seeing Jacob, and how to tell Kat about it if it did. Absently he found a plate and stood holding it.

Kat said in a strange, high voice, "What is the matter with you, anyhow? You're acting *weird*. Are you—are you mad at me or something? I—I can't help it if I can't see your little whatever-he-is! I—I—"

"Kat, of course I'm not mad!" Andy dumped his sandwich onto the plate and carried it to the table. *Now* who's not really looking, he asked himself severely. "Cool off, nothing's wrong, not really. I'm just *feeling* weird."

"Because of yesterday?"

"Yeah."

Kat picked up her sandwich and put it down again. "Why did you go down there without me this morning?" Before he could answer, she added quickly, "Did you see him?"

"Yeah."

She said nothing, only went pink-cheeked and picked up the sandwich again and began nibbling at the edges, not looking at Andy. He filled his mouth with melted cheese and charred toast. Probably the first thing to do was to tell her all about the conversation—what he had said, what Jacob had said. Then see what *she* said.

He began.

And of course what she said first of all was: "But I *did* really look! I tried and tried and tried and you know I did, so what am I not doing? I feel so—"

"Wait a minute, wait. I know you tried. Only maybe that's the trouble—all that *feeling*, or thinking about how you're feeling, or—" Andy broke off, despairing of ever getting it said. He didn't understand it very well himself. "Yesterday —and the time before when I saw him—you were mad at me. Remember?"

"Not the first time, though."

"That time you were busy listening to a tape."

"Well—! Of course I was busy! Music isn't just background noise! Not to me it isn't! I mean—"

"That's what I'm saying! What you were *really* looking at was *it*. And the two other times you were only seeing how yucky I was and how mad you were. So—you didn't see Jacob." There was a silence, instead of rebuttal. "Does that make sense?" he ventured.

"Yeah," Kat said. She was staring at him, blinking.

"Not that it matters, usually—I mean there's nothing wrong with it! I only want you to see Jacob so we both won't think *I'm* going nuts."

"And anyway I want to. And you think I could, if I—if I what, exactly?"

"I dunno," Andy told her, feeling helpless himself.

Kat, on the other hand, was beginning to pull herself together. She swallowed hard, and the pink flush faded into her normal freckle-sprinkled tan, and her mouth got its determined look. "I'm going to do it, too. I'm going to see him. I'll—I'll practice." She stood up suddenly, covered her eyes and turned her back to Andy. "You are wearing your brown-and-blue plaid shirt," she announced firmly. "And your old gray jeans, the ones with the pocket torn. Or . . . no . . . I guess . . ." She shot a glance at him and looked mortified.

"I'm not wearing 'em 'cause they're filthy," he told her. "Anyhow, clothes and thing don't matter—you were right."

Kat took her plate to the sink. "Yeah, but they're something I don't notice. I'm going to *learn* to. Keep asking me what color things are, and all that. I don't *want* to be always thinking about myself, or how I'm feeling, but I just get interested in seeing if I can figure out . . . "

Andy listened, counted fifteen *I's* and ten *me's* before he finished his lunch, and felt grave doubts about anything coming of his vague and probably useless plan.

However, after the kitchen was cleared and he'd changed out of his root-grubbing clothes, they headed for the forested hillside and down the shortcut.

"Listen, what if I still can't see him?" Kat asked nervously as she skidded down the slope in Andy's wake. "Should I say something, maybe? Like 'Hello, Jacob,' or—"

"I dunno—yes, maybe."

"I'd feel awfully dumb, though. Talking to that rock. To nobody."

Andy halted and faced her, braced with one leg downhill and the other up. "Try to believe there *is* somebody! Kat, there *is*."

"Okay," she said after a moment. "Okay, I'll try. I'll just keep telling myself—"

"Don't keep telling yourself anything! Look away, at something else. Think of something outside yourself."

"Like what?" They were stumbling and giant-stepping along again down the steepest part.

"Anything! That huckleberry bush. Those ferns, a cloud. That flicker!"

"What flicker?"

"The one that just flew from that tree trunk there. He's gone now."

"He was sitting on a *tree trunk*?"

"Flickers are kind of woodpeckers. He was probably hiding a nut or something. Never mind him, just—"

"Well, I don't have a bird book! But it's true, I didn't see him," Kat said sadly. "I'd probably have heard him, if he'd said something, but I never *look*. I don't think I ever saw a flicker in my whole, entire life."

"Well, it's no tragedy, you can see one in the next two or three minutes if you keep your eyes open," Andy retorted. "I'm sorry," he added immediately. "But the point is, quit *stewing* about it. Just start *looking*."

Kat said in a resolute voice, "Okay. I will."

She said nothing else as they reached the path and started down it, Andy still in the lead. His chest was beginning to feel funny, the way it did before a math test, and he was out of breath. Came down the slope too fast, he told himself, trying not to peer ahead to where the path ended at the corner of the old cemetery fence, and the graveled lane began—trying not to let his feet drag to put off the moment when the big rock would come into view.

The moment came in any case. Jacob was there, waiting. Andy halted, also waiting. Kat crunched up quietly behind him, standing so close he could feel her warmth on his elbow. She was silent for what seemed a long, long time.

Then, very softly, she said, "Oh."

Jacob was looking at her. "Hiyuh," he said in his husky voice.

"Hi," said Kat, barely audible.

Andy's chest expanded cautiously; he glanced around at her. She was smiling—at Jacob, not at him. He filled his lungs with summer air and let it all out in one great gusty *whoosh* of relief. "Well, thank the Lord," he said in his ordinary, back-to-normal tones. "*Now*. Can we get down to business about this *bed*?"

CHAPTER SEVEN

Andy had never seen Jacob's expression change from its usual wary, tired, or evasive look. But it changed now, to one of painful anxiety just tinged with eagerness and hope. It was as if a light had come on behind his thin little face. Andy suddenly noticed that his eyes were blue—deep blue, like a Christmas-card sky. And he was almost— not quite—beginning a smile; it flickered over his lips without really curving them, like a bird afraid to settle.

"You're going to get my bed back for me?" he asked Andy. "You really are?"

"I'm gonna try. I said I would, didn't I—if you let my sister see you."

"And I do see you," whispered Kat.

"Time for my part of the bargain now." Andy gestured expansively. A two-ton weight had fallen off his back in the last five minutes and the world had settled into its familiar unthreatening aspect. He *felt* expansive. "So—what do I do?"

"Get my bed back."

"Yeah, right. But how?"

Jacob said, "I don't know."

The sunshine in Andy's mind dimmed just slightly. "Well, now wait. I need a clue or two. Where is this bed? That's the first question."

"Around here," Jacob answered after a moment. "Well, I hope so. But I mean, who took it? How'd it happen?"

Jacob said, "I don't know." The light in his face, too, was dimming. "They just—stole it. It was mine."

"But—but—" Now, keep your cool, Andy cautioned himself. Just reason with him, find some way to . . . "You must know *something*," he said firmly. "Try, Jacob! If you don't tell me anything about it, what happened or anything, how am I going to help you?"

There was a silence. Jacob's face had faded into its old expression, but his gaze clung to Andy's. He said, "You promised."

And Kat said softly, "You did, you know."

"Yes, but—" Andy returned her look, perplexed. And naturally, when he turned back—

"Andy!" exclaimed Kat in a panic. "Andy, I can't see him anymore. I looked at you for just a *second*, and—"

"He's gone," Andy growled.

Turning his back on the big rock, he dropped down among the grass and weeds at the edge of the lane and stared off into the afternoon, elbows propped on knees, hands hanging clasped between them. After a moment Kat slowly sat down beside him, still looking uncertainly over her shoulder.

It was another moment before she said, "He's such a *little* boy. I—I thought he would be—different."

"I kept telling you he was just a little kid."

"I know, but—" Kat paused. "You said he was a weirdo and there was something funny about him, and . . . I didn't know I'd feel so sorry for him," she finished tremulously.

Andy glanced at her; she, too, was gazing over the hayfield, her profile fervent, and as expressive as a written sentence. He could tell right now that he was going to be getting that bed back for Jacob, somehow, someway, or she'd know the reason why.

He heaved a sigh and leaned back on his elbows. "What d'you make of him? Where does he *go* when he goes? And how does he do it so fast? That really bugs me!"

"I don't know, but you shouldn't get mad at him, Andy. *Poor* little thing!"

"Well, he keeps laying this on me! But he never tells me anything to help! I don't even know how to start."

"We have to figure it out."

"So go ahead, figure! I can't even figure out

where he comes from or what he is—I mean who he is."

Kat cut her eyes around toward him. "No. You mean *what* he is."

"Now listen, he's some kind of oddball little kid, that's what he is."

"*I* don't think so. I think he's a—a sort of little —wraith. The ghost of a little kid."

"Oh, have some sense!" said Andy loudly.

"That *is* sense." With a dramatic gesture Kat pointed uphill toward the weed-grown iron fence at the end of the lane. "What is that, right *there*? It's a cemetery! If your little kid's not a ghost why does he hang around a cemetery?"

"He doesn't! He hangs around an ordinary big rock clear on the other side of the lane and back almost to the woods. It's a good city block away."

"That's not very far. How do we know that isn't just—routine for ghosts? To stay a little ways away from their graves? In fact, it *is*. They don't sit there on their tombstones, they go haunt places!"

"Kat, come *on*. Ghosts don't exist!"

"They might. You don't know for sure any more than anybody else! I read a whole book once about old castles and things in England, where people have been seeing the very same ghosts looking the very same way for *hundreds* of years, and—"

"Oh, for the love of—if that's all the help you're going to be—"

"So where does he go, then? And how? You know good and well there's *no way* a real little kid could—just—disappear like that! You just tell me how one could."

Andy wriggled over onto his side, brushed away a sharp piece of gravel he'd been lying on, flung himself back again on his elbows, then sat up straight and sighed explosively. He had seldom felt so uncomfortable, inside and out. "Well, it's a really good trick!" he snapped at last. "I admit it. But that doesn't prove there's any such thing as *spooks* and neither does any dumb book full of stories about dumb English castles! People make up stuff, Kat. To scare themselves," he added, his voice steadying. It struck him he was probably onto something perfectly true, and reassuringly logical. "People like to be scared! Look at all the monster movies and everything. Way back in the Middle Ages people really believed all that stuff, so whenever some silly, hysterical old woman—"

"Why 'woman'?" Kat demanded sharply.

"—*or* man, *or* child—heard a screech owl or saw a sheet on the castle clothesline, they went telling everybody in town about this awful ghost, and from then on everybody that ever lived in that castle had to pretend to see the same thing or the castle's reputation'd be ruined, and—"

"Actually it's usually a Lady in Gray or the Third Earl who murdered his wife, and they're *in* the castle, not on the clothesline. And they always do the same thing—moan, or try to wash their hands, or—"

"Well, you know what I mean," Andy said. He was feeling much calmer, having found such a reasonable train of thought to follow, and Kat was nodding in an interested way. They were having a conversation now, not a fight.

Then Kat nearly ruined everything by saying, with a speculative look toward the iron fence, "We could go look around in there anyhow, though. See if there's a *Jacob* on any of those stones. Just in case."

"No!" Andy sprang to his feet. "We're not going to do any such stupid thing."

"Why not?"

"Because it's stupid!" He reached down and hauled Kat up too, and stared into her face a minute, then waved a wild hand around at the hay field, the lane, the hillside. "Look! This is just the plain, ordinary, modern world. We don't live in the Middle Ages. There's not a real castle anywhere in this country! And there's *no such thing as a ghost!*"

"No," Kat agreed, a little regretfully. She, too, surveyed the plain ordinary world and then glanced toward the rock. "Even if there are such things, surely Jacob wouldn't be one. He's not scary, he's—he's sweet."

"By the way, that's his name, Sweet," said Andy, suddenly realizing he'd never imparted this information. "Jacob Sweet. He told me so, about time-before-last. We could ask around." he added as they started on down the lane. "See if anybody knows him. I did ask Ellerton. This morning. Not by name, but—just if he'd ever seen a little kid like that."

"And I'll bet he hadn't," Kat said at once.

"Well, *that* doesn't prove anything!" Andy retorted. "He did say he'd seen kids up there—though not very often. I figure Jacob might even have spoken to him, and he just didn't hear."

"That could be," Kat admitted. "Or maybe he wasn't *really looking*." She thought a minute, then added with one of her flashes of X-ray vision, "I think Ellerton's more interested in poultry than in people."

"Let's ask Mr. Buckle. I kept meaning to and forgetting. Then—yesterday—" Andy smiled with with relief, glad the am-I-crazy? part was over. "We'll ask him now. He'll know Jacob by name. If he lives anywhere around here."

"And if he's a real live boy," added Kat.

"You wait and see," Andy told her.

But Mr. Buckle for once let him down. As soon as they'd been down to the poultry house for the Sunday-breakfast eggs, they searched him out and put their question. He pondered, working neat's-

foot oil into a piece of harness with his thick callused fingers as he squinted across the tack room
of the equipment barn, where they had found him.

"Jacob. Hmm. Kinda rings a bell, but . . . Nope,
don't think I do," he said at last with a shake of
his head. "I know a Jamie Sweet. And two Jacks.
But no Jacob, I guess. Maybe you got the name
wrong?"

The twins spoke together, Andy saying, "Uh—
I don't think so," and Kat saying, "Yes, maybe."
They exchanged a look, and Kat deftly changed the
subject by exclaiming, "Wow, what a lot of harness! Do you use all that for just Bonnie and
Clyde?" She swung around to peer at the walls of
the high, narrow room, which were festooned from
splintered floor to raftered ceiling with heavy
black straps of every length and width—brass
studded, nickel studded, one even silver trimmed—
draped over long wooden pegs.

"Oh, I drive half a dozen others," Mr. Buckle
told her. "Depends what they're pulling. They
kinda specialize, you know. F'instance, I've got a
top-notch ladies' cart horse. . . . "

Andy hadn't been ready for the subject to be
changed. Kat might think she'd now proved that
Jacob was nobody but a spook; Andy thought all
they'd proved was that Mr. Buckle didn't know
him. But before he could pursue that, the conversation had moved on, to Mrs. Buckle's collection of

blue ribbons, and the six-horse hitch Mr. Buckle showed with his fire engine. . . .

"Fire engine?" Andy echoed, his attention caught.

"Sure, I got a fire engine. Right in this barn." Mr. Buckle screwed the cap on his oil can and got up. "Come on. I'll show you."

The fire engine turned out to be the brass-trimmed scarlet wagon the twins had once glimpsed through the open barn door. It stood back in the dim interior now, impressive still with its big cylindrical tank and brass-nozzled hose, though Andy was glad he didn't live in the days when you'd have to depend on it if the house caught fire. Dreamily he trailed Mr. Buckle and Kat through the cool, straw-smelling, dusky space, watching the dust motes whirl in the occasional spear of sunlight that had found a chink between boards, feeling like somebody in a time-warp movie. They walked past high-wheeled wagons and buggies, a jaunty little cart with its whip sticking up, another with fringe on its top that had to be a surrey— and all polished and oiled like a this-year's Chevy, looking just as they must have looked to the people who used them a hundred or more years ago.

People like those old pioneers in the graveyard, came a thought slipping into his mind like one of the sun's thin knives—so unexpectedly it made him shiver. He pushed it out again, but recess was over; his mind was back on Jacob and his conscience jabbing him. He found a break in Kat's spate of questions and said they'd better quit bothering Mr. Buckle and go.

"No bother," Mr. Buckle assured him as they started back through the barn's dim reaches toward the big bright square of outdoors framed by the doorway. "I like kids. Got none of my own— mebbe that's why I keep borrowin' the neighbors'." He smiled at Kat. "I guess I know every kid for miles around—exceptin' your Jacob Sweet." He broke off abruptly, snapped his fingers. "By golly. No wonder that name rang a bell."

Andy's heart gave a thump and began beating in an unusual sort of way. Kat said, "You mean you do know a Jacob?"

"Why, sure! I forgot this kid because everybody calls him 'J.B.' But his name's Jacob—Jacob Benson Sweet. His mama's housekeeper up to the Lodge."

"Oh. Yeah. Mrs. Sweet," said Kat. She was plainly disappointed that everything was going to turn out perfectly normal after all.

"Dawnelle's mother," Andy said. When Mr. Buckle nodded he went on, "Was this—was J.B. here that day we drove?"

"No, he hurt his foot last weekend, Dawnelle told me. He usually comes. Were you wanting to see him about something?"

"Not really," Kat said quickly.

At the same moment, Andy said, "Yes."

We've got to quit doing that, Andy thought, feeling his ears heat up. But before he could think of an explanation. Mr. Buckle grinned and said, "Well, you fight it out. I better get back to my saddle soaping."

He turned away toward the tack room with his little farewell salute. Andy waved a response and started rapidly out of the barnyard, hurrying Kat along. The moment they were out of earshot he said triumphantly, "I know where Mrs. Sweet lives! It's no more'n a quarter of a mile from here. Let's go hunt up this J.B. right now. See if he's our Jacob."

Kat pulled her elbow out of his grasp. "If you'd just *described* ours to Mr. Buckle we'd know already!"

"Rather find out for myself," Andy said, and was glad when Kat made one of her door-slamming exits into a tape instead of arguing. She was just cross because she was wrong. He didn't want to argue, or hear any more of her doubting opinions. He didn't want to ask anybody else about Jacob, or describe him, or examine his own misgivings. He just wanted to *find* the kid and get it over with, and relax.

They'd nearly reached the county road when Kat pushed up one earphone and said, "Where is this place?"

"Almost straight across the road from the foot of this lane. The Christmas tree farm."

"*Christmas tree* farm?"

Naturally, she'd never noticed there was one. "I'll show you when we get there," Andy told her. He tucked the Sunday-breakfast egg cartons under a hazel bush to collect on the way back, and led the way across the road. Just a few more minutes, he was assuring himself.

But at the mailbox labeled "Martin Sweet' Kat hung back. "If it *is* our Jacob, he's Dawnelle's brother. D'you think some of those other kids might be there?"

"Dawnelle might be there. She lives there," Andy pointed out reasonably. "Come on—she won't bite!"

Kat gave a reluctant giggle and quit resisting. They walked in silence between plantings of all the kinds of trees Andy used to sell at Christmas for the Scouts: waist-high Noble fir on their left, taller blue spruce on their right, some native Douglas firs farther along. Easy sort of crop to raise, Andy thought. Just keep down the weeds and let it grow. The house, which was old and narrow-shouldered and gleaming white, was backed by a mix of juniper and huge dark holly trees. The whole place smelled of Christmas and December; you could almost hear the bells of the street-corner Santas. It was strange to smell that on a summer afternoon.

There was a front walk, slightly grass-grown. While Kat lingered nervously on it, Andy marched straight up the steps to the door and knocked. After a moment, he discovered a worn brass handle, like a clock-winding key, and twirled it for good measure. It trilled loudly. Nothing further happened. He was beginning to say "Nobody home. I s'pose Mr. Sweet's out carpentering, and Mrs. Sweet—" when behind him, Kat whispered, "Andy!"

He turned to see Dawnelle peering at them from around the corner of the house. She emerged awkwardly, with an air of relief. "Oh. Hi. I didn't know who . . . Nobody ever uses that door— only the kitchen."

"Sorry," Andy muttered. He came back down the steps, wondering for the first time exactly how to state their errand. "We . . . uh . . . I mean, Mr. Buckle told us . . . " He stopped. "Is J.B. around?"

"Oh. Sure. He's out in the barn," Dawnelle waved a hand toward the back of the house, her black-lashed turquoise eyes flicking a self-conscious glance at Kat, who murmured "Thanks" and started hastily in the direction she had pointed. As she passed, Dawnelle ventured a small, cautious smile; Kat responded in kind. *Progress*, reflected Andy as he followed. Eventually—say six months or so, when they both relaxed—they might even get to be friends.

The barn, like Mr. Buckle's, was loftly, dim, and shafted with streaks of sun full of dancing dust motes. Unlike his, it smelled of machine oil and fresh wood—not horses. The gangling shapes of disks and harrows crowded the shadows, along with a couple of flatbed trailers. In the space near the big open doors, the   sun spotlighted a bright orange tractor. A man leaning over the tractor's engine straightened and turned inquiringly as they approached.

They shopped short. It wasn't a man—just a tall boy, of fourteen or fifteen. He had intensely black hair and eyes like Dawnelle's—and one foot in a bedroom slipper.

Andy's heart plummeted. "You're J.B.?" he managed to ask.

"That's right," said the boy, and waited.

Now what do I say? Andy asked himself in sudden confusion. He hadn't thought this far. He shifted his feet, glanced over his shoulder at Kat, who was smiling a cat's smile at the floor, then faced the boy again. "Sorry. We were trying to find a—a Jacob Sweet. But you're not the right one."

J.B. looked puzzled. "I thought I was the only one around here—except my dad's uncle, lives in Portland. You don't mean Jack?"

Andy shook his head and plodded through a description of Jacob, but there was no sign of recognition on J.B.'s face, though he was friendly enough, and offered to ask his dad. Andy thanked him, mumbled another apology, and the twins got themselves off the property and back to the road.

"What did I tell you?" Kat remarked with maddening satisfaction as they started for the Lodge.

At the cost of some effort, Andy made no reply.

He managed to remember to retrieve the eggs as they went up the Buckles' lane. And when they passed the big rock he managed to glance toward it only casually, without expectation.

Just as well. There wasn't a sign of Jacob.

CHAPTER EIGHT

That evening over dinner (another duck-egg omelet, with muffins; pretty good) they told Dodie about the driving lessons. They also talked about Mr. Buckle, and the old fire engine, and Mrs. Buckle's cowboy boots and blue horse-show ribbons, and the guinea hens and Ellerton. They even mentioned the Christmas tree farm and the Sweet family's Siamese cat eyes. But they didn't say a word about Jacob.

"Why didn't we?" Kat said thoughtfully, when Dodie had left for her nightly check of the Lodge and they were clearing the dishes.

Andy, who had been wondering too, attempted to shrug it off. "Nothing much to tell, is there? She probably wouldn't be interested."

"You mean she might be *too* interested," Kat retorted as if she could read his mind. "She'd want to go down and see for herself, and ask Jacob questions. And what if she *couldn't* see him?"

"Yeah, that's the trouble with Jacob," Andy muttered. "We can't even see him ourselves whenever we want."

They exchanged a glance and needed no further

discussion. There were a good many things—or kinds of things—one didn't confide to Dodie, unless one was prepared for an alert but sometimes uncomfortably sharp cross-questioning, or an expert debunking followed by a warning against confusing sense with nonsense. Best keep Jacob a private matter until something further developed— if anything did.

On Sunday morning, Mrs. Corey-who-cooks opened the refrigerator door, saw the unfamiliar egg cartons, and reacted exactly as Kat had predicted.

"Where'd *these* come from? Buckles'! Never heard their eggs were a minute fresher than anybody else's. What's the matter with Len's, all of a sudden, I'd like to know?" When Dodie, who was peering into cupboards checking staples, chose to consider the question rhetorical, she added belligerently, "This Lodge been doing business with Harper's Poultry Farm ever since it opened. You folks got somethin' against my brother-in-law? Don't like his manners, maybe? Think his place is dirty?"

"Yes," said Dodie baldly.

Kat, eavesdropping from the next room as she set the breakfast tables, reported this scene verbatim to Andy later. "Andy, you should've *heard* her! Dodie's *brave*."

"Well, after all, she's the boss," remarked Andy, unimpressed. "So did Mrs. Corey quit, or what?"

But Mrs. Corey only quit being predictable. For a moment she simply stood and looked at Dodie, then she laughed—richly and with enjoyment. "You're right," she said. "It's dirty as a pigpen and Len Harper's the rudest man in this county. How my sister's stood him all these years I'll never know. Well, serves him right, the old galoot. Teach him to go around thinking he owns the earth and runs that town."

"That's what she said!" Kat finished.

"What d'you know," Andy said with a grin.

"But she said something else." Uneasiness flitted over Kat's face like a cloud shadow over a field. "She said, 'You probably made a enemy, though. Len holds a grudge.' And she wasn't laughing then."

Andy thought about this a moment, a bit uncomfortable himself. "So let him hold it," he told Kat. "He can't hurt us. Just forget it."

This turned out to be hard in a place like Harper's Mill, where everybody knew your business as soon as you did, found it interesting—and took sides. A couple of days later, when he and Kat walked to town on their routine errands, they found themselves bathed in unaccustomed limelight. People who would scarcely have given them a glance last week now turned to stare after them, with expressions ranging from grins to scowls.

At Harper's Supermarket an especially alert silence fell over the lineup at the checkout stand the moment they came in, and Mrs. Harper, at the cash register, was distinctly heard to remark that she was glad the Lodge hadn't transferred *all* its business to competitors. To this the butcher—Mrs. Corey's nephew Bob—retorted that it was lucky the store *had* no competitors within thirty miles. Both remarks drew snickers from customers—though not from the same ones. At the post office, nice Mr. Edwin Harper the postmaster stated his opinion that it was a free country and folks ought to do business where it suited them. Reverend Frank Mahaffey, the new and very young minister of the Congregational Church, warmly agreed with him. However, a Mr. Jenkins waiting his turn at the stamp window spoke up with some heat to point out that the Buckles' business was supposed to be horses, not eggs, and there wasn't room hereabouts for two poultry operations. The Reverend Mahaffey hastily agreed with him, too. The widow Maria Corey added disparagingly that it was only to give that Ellerton Clark some busywork to do, and drew fire from a Mrs. Millard Sweet—secretary of the church's Ladies' Guild—who hotly defended Ellerton and private enterprise, reducing the Reverend Mahaffey to uneasy silence.

Plainly, the town had split into three separate camps: Len Harper conservatives, pro-Lodge liberals, and interested neutrals waiting to see what happened next. All this about *eggs*, Andy thought in disbelief.

"What else do they *think*'ll happen?" he demanded as he and Kat started back up the road. "The show's all over."

"What if it isn't, though?" Kat asked, big eyed. "What if that yucky Mr. Harper does something to get even? Like—like burn down the Lodge!"

"Oh, don't be silly," scoffed Andy.

Kat put up her earphones and stalked on.

He could silence her, but not the uncomfortable little squirming of guilt he kept feeling about bringing all this hostility down upon the Buckles and even Ellerton. That afternoon, when he and Kat went down for their first private driving lesson, he apologized to Mr. Buckle, needing to get the whole thing out in the open. To his vast relief, Mr. Buckle laughed it off, saying old Len Harper always had been the sourest man in the state of Oregon, and must have been raised on lemons instead of mother's milk.

"You should've heard the carryings-on a few years back about some fool parade the town was fixing to have. The mayor—that was Ed Harper the postmaster, then—he came up to the house one day and arranged with me to hitch up a team to that antique fire wagon, and lead the parade. Nifty idea, seemed to me. Turned out Len figured *he'd* lead the parade in his new Buick. I thought the town might go to civil war over that one. Don't you worry, Myra 'n me, we're used to it," he assured Andy. "We're still foreigners around here— only lived here forty years. Any time they need somebody to pick on, they pick on us. This'll blow over in a couple of weeks."

Andy could only hope he was right.

Dodie held herself majestically above the fracas, referring to it as *"l'affaire* Egg" and remarking indifferently that the village must amuse itself as it could. She *was* pretty brave, Andy reflected, observing a side of her he seldom saw—the redoubtable Dorothy Peterson who had once made ends meet while juggling a job, a Master's thesis, and preschool-age twins—who regularly took on Campion Hall's headmaster, and who had been described by a faculty colleague as "a formidable lady." Probably her French students knew that Dodie very well. Andy was rather glad that he did not. The Dodie he knew best was a funnier, quirkier, and altogether more comfortable person to have around—and he and Kat preferred to keep her so. For unsafe subjects they had each other— one of the advantages, they had learned, of being twins.

With the writers gone and the weather turned

wet and chilly, Dodie was around much more in the next few days, getting the cottage to suit her and organizing the rest of the summer. Andy learned that he had much to accomplish on the various nature trails before the next group— eighteen landscape artists and their teacher—arrived the following Thursday evening.

"After they're gone, we've got a free week before that senior citizens group descends on us." Dodie paused, tapping her pencil against her teeth and studying the calendar. "I'll have to spend a day or two in Portland, getting Mr. Handy started on our roof. Come what may, that's got to be re-shingled."

"You're going to Portland? Can't we come?" cried Kat—then added immediately, "Oh, but I don't want to miss the driving lessons."

Andy had swallowed a similar exclamation. While Dodie was explaining why it was impossible that they all be gone at once, he wandered over to the window to peer out restlessly into the dripping world. Days like this—and the Fourth of July had been one of them, canceling their picnic plans and the second driving lesson—he missed Phil Darling and his other friends in Portland pretty bad. But he had only to consider leaving and his thoughts snapped back here as if tethered by rubber bands— to Mr. Buckle and the horses, and the infinite amount he wanted to learn from the one about the other, to the emerging trails which had somehow become his private, personal project . . . and of course, to Jacob. Nagging, baffling, unfinished business, all left up in the air.

Jacob's absence was beginning to be more nerve-racking than his presence had been. He hadn't shown himself once since the Saturday when Kat had managed to *really look*—nearly a week ago. Every time the two of them walked down that path they dawdled, watched for him—and saw only an empty clearing. It seemed *extra* empty. Even the big rock had begun to look somehow derelict, abandoned, as if he weren't *ever* going to come back now. Absently tying one-handed knots in the curtain pull, Andy wondered if it had something to do with Kat—if he should have kept the whole thing just between him and Jacob. But Jacob hadn't minded Kat's knowing . . . that wasn't the problem. The wet weather wasn't, either. Andy suspected he knew very well what the problem was: Jacob had quit believing he'd keep his promise. The light that had come on briefly behind those sky-blue eyes, then slowly faded—it haunted him. Kat, too. "We've got to *do* something," she kept telling Andy. But he noticed she never said *what*.

She came up beside him, stared glumly at the rain, and said, "I wish we had our piano, so I could get that fugue."

"Well, that's a new one," Dodie remarked. "At

home, your theme song is 'If only I didn't have to do Bach!' "

"I didn't say I *liked* it. I just don't want to go to music camp without it *perfect*. I'd look like a dummy."

"You'll look like Vladimir Horowitz beside some of those kids, *mon petit prodige*. I wouldn't worry." Dodie made a final note on her calendar, then tossed it aside and stood up. "So. There goes July. Maybe in August we can lie around with our feet up. Who wants chili for lunch?"

The rain stopped Friday morning, but the creek trail was still a bog. Letting the day of warmth and drier air go to work on it, Andy went down to the Buckles' with Kat for another session with the horses. Mr. Buckle had started them driving Bonnie alone, hitched to a light four-wheeled cart with just room for him and one twin on the forward seat, the other twin in back. It wasn't quite as exciting, sitting close behind one horse instead of perched up high above two with four reins to control—and just driving sedately up and down the lane instead of bouncing around on the pasture. But it wasn't as hair-raising, either. With their very first private lesson Kat had relaxed and begun to learn. This second one she actually enjoyed, and Andy could forget her and concentrate dotingly on Bonnie.

Over the weekend he shifted his attentions to the less overgrown west trail, before returning

Monday to the creek. The dry weather held and by
Wednesday noon he was sure of getting that one,
too, in passable shape by Dodie's Thursday dead-
line. He declared a vacation. After lunch he and
Kat slithered down the still soggy hill for their
third private drive.

Kat instantly destroyed his holiday mood by
asking if he'd done anything yet about Jacob.

"Now when have I had time to do anything
about *anything* in I-don't-know-when?"

"Well, I did something this morning. I asked
Mrs. Corey-who-cooks if there'd ever been a ghost
around this neighborhood."

Andy turned so quickly he nearly lost his foot-
ing, and had to grab a tree trunk. "Kat! She'll think
you're out of your skull."

"Well, she didn't. She only laughed and said I'd
have to ask old Aunt Henry, because spooks and
suchlike ought to be right down her alley."

"Who's old Aunt Henry?"

"Dawnelle's father's great-aunt, I think. I suppose it's 'Henrietta,' really. Anyway she's about
ninety and lives all by herself in a little house on
their farm and has ten cats."

"Sounds like some kind of spook herself. You
should've asked Mrs. Corey if she's ever seen
Jacob."

"Same question," Kat retorted. "Anyway, she
wouldn't have. She never comes down this way,

she drives around by the road. We ought to ask Mr. Buckle again. We only asked him if he knew a Jacob Sweet," she went on loudly, overriding Andy's objection. "Not if he's ever seen *ours*."

True. But something inside Andy was pulling back—it pulled back now every time he thought of mentioning Jacob in any way, to anybody. "He probably hasn't seen him," he muttered.

"I'll bet he has. He must come past here all the time—it's his property! Besides, Mr. Buckle's somebody who *really looks*."

That was true, too. Mr. Buckle had perceived at once how Andy felt about being the mammoth twin, seen right through Kat's pride to her timidity near the big horses. He was a close observer. And when you told him something he listened.

Kat had been following her own, perhaps similar, train of thought. She went on, "We could even ask him if he'd ever heard of a stolen bed. He wouldn't laugh or think we were dumb or anything. I know he wouldn't. We *could* ask Dawnelle and J.B., too. They were kind of—nice, didn't you think so? . . . Wait, Andy, let's walk slow."

"He won't be there." Andy sighed. Still, they stood staring toward the big crouching rock until its loneliness oppressed them, and a chickadee's repeated *dee-dee-dee*ing from the graveyard fence grated like a fingernail on the blackboard.

"I wish he'd come back," Kat said plaintively as

they started on. "I've only seen him *once.* Anyway I've got a question I want to ask him."

"Save your breath," Andy told her. "I've asked him a dozen he wouldn't answer."

"But this one's not personal or anything. I just want to ask him to describe that bed."

Andy, who had been racking his brain to think of something—anything—that Jacob wouldn't mind telling them, considered this and said, "What for?"

"Well, now listen," Kat said carefully. "Don't say anything till I've finished. What if—pretend this for just one second—what if Jacob *is* a ghost? —maybe a little pioneer Sweet, buried in that old graveyard right back there?"

"Kat, *what* is the sense in . . . Okay, okay, I'll pretend. So what if he is?"

"Well, *a,* he'd be a sort of long-ago relative of J.B. and Dawnelle's so *b,* they might know about this bed!"

Andy gaped at her. "How did you get from *a* to *b*? Or am I supposed to pretend that, too?"

"No! They'd know because it'd be part of their family history! I mean, it must've been some really special bed—maybe carried all the way across the plains in a covered wagon or something, a kind of heirloom, or . . . or maybe with a secret hiding place in one of the bedposts where the family jewels were hidden—"

"The Sweet family brought *diamonds* and things across those plains?"

"Well, they might've, mightn't they?"

"And they'd let this little nine-year-old have the bed with the family fortune in it?"

"Oh, don't be so—so—"

"Sensible," supplied Andy. "Okay, okay," he added hastily, to ward off the explosion. "I don't mind asking Jacob to describe it. As soon as we get a chance."

"If we ever get another chance," Kat said reproachfully.

"Listen, it's not *my* fault he's staying away like this!"

"Well, he thinks you're getting his bed back! So he's just waiting. You did promise," she added as they walked on.

Andy didn't answer.

Today Clyde went between the buggy's shafts, and after a circle of the barnyard and one trip down the lane, Mr. Buckle asked Kat if she was ready to try the pasture. "Won't be near as rough as it was in that old wagon," he told her. "This thing's pretty well sprung."

"I'm not scared," she said crisply, and drove on up the lane to the corner, guided Clyde neatly around it and along past the graveyard's tall open gates.

As they went by Andy caught a flash of movement and craned back to see a familiar slight figure waving to them. "It's Ellerton," he said, and waved back.

"Probably fighting blackberry around the fence," remarked Mr. Buckle. "Him and that blackberry's got a real war on, but I think Ellerton'll win it. Now take it easy here, Kat honey, till you get the turn made into the field. Going to bounce around some."

"I bet Ellerton knows all the names on all the graves," Kat said in a thoughtful voice that made Andy wish he'd merely waved and kept his mouth shut.

"Yep, he likely does," agreed Mr. Buckle. "Keep that right rein good and firm, Kat, ol' Clyde's trying to cut corners on you. Make him take 'em square. . . ."

Andy drove the other two sides of the pasture, keeping his corners square and taking the uphill grade at a trot—and as usual, it felt like homecoming, like the one thing he'd been waiting all his life to do. But he wished he could fling himself into it the way he'd done that very first day. Every time since, he'd felt divided, as he did today—torn between his eagerness to learn everything there was to learn about driving Belgians, and his nagging burden of responsibility about some *bed*. This Jacob business was somehow putting everything else on "hold."

By the time he'd driven another circuit and back

past the graveyard the gates were closed and Ellerton was nowhere in sight. Trying not to notice the feeling of reprieve this gave him, Andy began rehearsing ways to find out if Mr. Buckle had ever seen Jacob. Kat would of course leave it up to him.

But it was Mr. Buckle, after all, who opened the touchy subject. "You two ever find J.B.?" he asked as he undid the traces and led Clyde free of the shafts.

'Oh, yes!" said Kat. "But—"

"But he wasn't the person we—had in mind," Andy finished. Then, receiving a glance like a hard nudge in the ribs from Kat, he plunged in. "The thing is, Mr. Buckle, we keep seeing this boy around that path up there—little kid, about nine years old. . . ." He began to describe Jacob, but even before he was through, Mr. Buckle was nodding.

"Yeah, I've noticed that kid now and then—or one mighty like him."

Andy filled his lungs in relief and satisfaction. So he'd been right all along—Jacob *was* just an ordinary kid. Feeling more relaxed than he had for a week, he asked, "D'you know where he lives?"

"Don't even know who he is," Mr. Buckle said. "Known him by sight for years, but—" he broke off, a very odd expression passing over his features. After a moment he added, "Probably isn't the same kid. They all look a lot alike at that age." He stopped again, then said abruptly, "Why're you asking? What about him?"

Disconcerted, Andy stumbled over his answer, all his misgivings flooding back. "We—we were gonna ask *you*. I mean . . . he says his name is Jacob Sweet, that's why we . . . And he's got some yarn about somebody ripping off his bed. That's all we know about him."

"And he's from 'around here,' " Kat added.

They waited, uneasily watching Mr. Buckle, who had listened with close attention but with his gaze on the ground, his rugged, heavy-jawed face now quite impassive. In an equally neutral voice he asked, "Whereabouts on that path did you see him?"

"Not really *on* the path—up above it, and back toward the woods—near that great big rock."

"Yeah, Beaver Rock," said Mr. Buckle. He was silent a moment, then went on in his easy, every-day manner, as if he were explaining the function of a piece of harness. "That's an old landmark hereabouts. Indians named it, way back when. I guess the thing looked like a beaver to them. Pioneers took up the name, and it stuck."

He paused as if expecting somebody to say something, so Andy mumbled, "I thought it looked like a dog or something myself." It seemed to him Mr. Buckle was changing the subject—and hoping they wouldn't notice. It was the sort of thing your plain ordinary grown-ups did.

He was going right on with it, too. "Yeah, got a real distinctive shape," he agreed, as if any of them really cared. "Kind of thing they used to mark boundaries by—'hundred yards due north from the fallen tree, west to Beaver Rock.' Matter of fact I think it's mentioned on my deed. My property line runs just this side of it." He smiled. Then he glanced at his watch, said, "Oh-oh!" and backed a step toward the house. "Say, I hate to run you off, but I promised Mrs. Buckle I'd ride old Velvet down to the blacksmith's today and git 'er some new shoes. She's been actin' kinda ouchy. You come back any time, now." He smiled again, gave his little salute, and strode quickly toward the house.

Andy and Kat stared after him, exchanged a long look, and silently turned away.

"He never really answered us," Andy said finally as they started up the lane. "How come? You don't suppose he was mad or something?" He was feeling as though he couldn't stand it if they had offended Mr. Buckle. Or embarrassed him or anything. But if they had, he couldn't imagine how.

"He didn't act *mad*," Kat said. "Just—kind of funny."

"Real funny. He sort of . . . brushed us off. But

why? He never—dodged—like that before. I didn't think he *would*."

"I didn't either," Kat said disconsolately.

After a minute she fumbled for a tape, put her earphones up and retreated into her reliable private world. Andy wished he had one. At the rock, they hesitated only briefly before plodding on up the path, Andy staring at the trodden weeds and pinkish dirt beneath his feet, hearing the jingling little tambourines of Kat's music and his own puffing as they labored up the hillside shortcut, which seemed for the first time wearisome and long.

He never knew whether it was some other sound or merely chance that made him turn, just before they reached the trees, to glance back over his shoulder. Quickly he caught Kat's arm, and pointed.

Down there on the path below was Mr. Buckle, mounted bareback on one of the big horses—but not yet on his way to Harper's Mill and the blacksmith. He was sitting motionless, wrists crossed upon the saddle horn, gazing intently up toward Beaver Rock.

CHAPTER NINE

"He *has*. He must've," Kat insisted next day for the dozenth time since breakfast. It was mid-morning, bright and cloudless, getting hot even on the shaded creek trail. Andy had been working without a shirt. At the moment he was sitting on a mossy log beside Kat, drinking the pop she'd brought down to relieve his thirst, *she* said; he thought it was mainly to carry on the argument they'd been having since the afternoon before.

"He never actually said he'd seen Jacob," Andy repeated stubbornly.

"Well, he had. He recognized him!"

"All he said was 'one mighty like him.' Could've been some other kid. They *do* all kind of look alike at that age." Andy was tired and feeling as if a dark cloud had come over his personal sky; it made him obstinate.

Kat demanded, "Then why did he act so funny, and stop in the middle of talking to us? Why did he ride up there to the rock?"

"I don't know. There could be lots of reasons."

"He knows something we don't. *That's* the reason."

"He knows lots of things we don't! Including stuff that's none of our business." Even Andy could see that he wasn't making much sense. Plainly, Mr. Buckle not only knew something they didn't, but didn't want to discuss it—at least not with them. Well, he had a perfect right, of course. Naturally. After all, to him they were barely acquaintances—just a couple more kids. Nothing special at all. *So get that through your head*, Andy told himself angrily.

Kat merely took a swallow of pop and stared thoughtfully at the bottle. "It was something we said that made him . . . that changed him."

Andy, too, had been trying his best to pin down exactly what the change had been. "Surprised him?" he hazarded.

"Not 'surprised,' exactly. I think it scared him."

"Mr. Buckle scared!" Andy flung her an impatient look. "I'll believe that when I see it."

"I think we *did* see it. You just don't want to believe it. You never believe things! You wouldn't believe a thing if it was under your nose!"

"Oh, come on. Like what?"

"Like a grave with Jacob's name on it. *You're* scared of *that*. You don't even want to go and look! I'm lots braver than you are. Lots."

"Then why don't you go by yourself and look?" snapped Andy, goaded to the end of his patience.

"Well, I would! Only . . . only . . ."

Only she *was* a little scared, thought Andy. Just wouldn't admit it.

". . . only you'd just say I was making it up!" she finished defiantly.

Andy finished his pop, stood up, and handed her the bottle. "Thanks, that was good. I have to get back to work now," he said with dignity.

"Ohhhhhhhh," Kat growled under her breath. She grabbed the bottle and took herself off up the trail and back to her napkin counting.

Andy returned to his grubbing and his gloom, silently continuing the argument. *He* was not at all scared of finding anybody's name on any gravestone, or of going to look, or—or anything else. Because—point number one: What was there to be scared of? Ghosts didn't exist. He was *reluctant*, yes. Because—well, point number two: That cemetery was private property, Harper's Mill Historical Society property, and not supposed to be wandered around in by just anybody. Why else was that fence around it? And big strong gates, usually closed. And anyway—point number three: It was a graveyard. It belonged to the people in the graves. And point number four: If Mr. Buckle had recognized Jacob from their description it was because he'd seen a real live little kid, which proved point number one, so there was no need for anybody else to prove it.

Andy thought a while longer, but couldn't find

point number five, or much comfort in any of the others, only a stronger and stronger feeling that he did not want to go through those tall iron gates.

By noon the creek trail was almost finished—but his gloom lingered, dimming his pleasure as he walked back along the freshly raked, fern-fringed path on his way to the cottage. Nor was the argument, he had to admit, much nearer to being settled. Uncomfortably aware that his own position on the ghost matter was rapidly shifting into a corner, he brought the subject up himself at the lunch table with misplaced bravado, in order to defend the right of any intelligent person to doubt anything he couldn't see with his own eyes. "Besides, suppose we did see a gravestone—one with 'Jacob Sweet' written right on it—that wouldn't mean *our* Jacob is some dumb little ghost. It wouldn't mean anything at all!"

"No, I guess it wouldn't," Kat said after a moment, with a mildness that instantly put him on his guard. "In fact, it's just what I've been saying: Seeing and believing don't really have much to do with each other."

"*That's* what you've been saying?" Andy retorted with a stare.

"Sure. There's lots of things you don't have to see to believe. Hundreds and hundreds of 'em."

"Name three."

"Music," Kat shot back. "Electricity. Cold. Heat. A pane of glass."

"Oh, *well*! You can't *see* those, maybe. But you can sure hear them or feel them! I meant—"

"You *said* 'see,' " Kat pointed out maddeningly. "All right, then—radio waves. Television signals. Carbon dioxide fumes. Dodie's perfume."

Andy, suddenly conscious of the faint, familiar fragrance that was always part of wherever they lived, scrambled distractedly for a reply, and Kat got in ahead of him.

"And there's things you can't *touch* that you've got to believe. Like color. Like light. Or sound. Or—or excitement. Or stars."

"Now wait a minute! We could touch stars, all right. If we were close enough—and had fireproof fingers."

"Maybe so and maybe not! Some stars are only big swirls of gas, not fire or rocks or anything solid at all. And some of 'em burnt out ages and ages ago, and all we see is leftover light that's just now reaching us after about a jillion years. We still *see* them—but they're not even there!" Triumphant, Kat returned to her soup. "I took science last semester, remember?"

"Too bad," Andy muttered.

"And I read that library book—that one about cells and things. Yes, and if you want to talk about *cells*, and microorganisms and—"

"Well, I *don't* want to talk about them!" Andy
flung down his spoon with a clatter, took his bowl
to the sink, then headed for the door. He'd had
enough to eat. He'd had enough yakking. He ought
to know better than to argue with Kat; she always
won. Which did *not* mean, he told himself force-
fully as he stalked across the clearing, that she was
always right. She couldn't be right about this. Some
things existed and some did not. Ghosts did not. All
you needed was your *common* sense to tell you
that. He'd never seen a ghost before, had he?

All of a sudden that possible Great Truth he'd
discovered a while back about Uncle Richard—
*since such a thing never had happened to him, he
just figured it never would*—sailed back home like
a boomerang to hit him hard. Who was figuring
that way now?

Finding himself standing beside the bench in
front of The Annex, he dropped down heavily upon it. There he sat in silence, listening to the little
tinhorn voices of a couple of nuthatches busy
among the fir cones, until his anger died its usual
early death. It was replaced by a miserable feeling
of being pushed onto quicksand, for he could not
rid himself of the sneaking suspicion that this time
Kat might be right. At least partially. What she'd
said about the old stars—burnt out a million years
ago and still visible. Suppose it were something
like that with Jacob? Suppose they'd really seen

him—but he wasn't really there? Where did that leave "seeing" and "believing"?

He couldn't begin to answer that. He wished he'd never thought of it.

What was more, he resolved firmly after a moment, he wasn't about to suppose any such thing. It would mean admitting that the world he'd always felt right at home in was actually some unfamiliar, unreliable sort of booby trap where you couldn't count on anything. And that couldn't be so.

Kat presently appeared at his elbow, handed him a doughnut, and without comment joined him on the bench. For a few minutes they sat in silence, chewing, letting the frayed edges between them mend. A flash of brilliance high in a fir tree caught Andy's attention. It was followed by a brief stanza of rather hoarse flute music—like a robin with a cold. The bird sailed down to a lower branch and Kat gasped.

"Oh, look! That red and yellow! D'you see?"

He nodded, shifting the last of the doughnut into one cheek. "Western tanager," he said around it.

"Oh, you and your bird book! Someday I'm going to see something before you do," Kat muttered.

"At least you saw it."

"I heard it. So then I looked."

"Oh. That figures." Andy turned to her, momentarily diverted. "I look. You *hear*. I'll bet you could even repeat that song."

Kat squinted a second, then said, "E, E-flat, E, F. With grace notes after each one."

Andy, who had expected her to try whistling the phrase—as he'd often done with no success at all—was reduced to wishing he hadn't got the only tin ear in the family, and wondering what it was like inside Kat's head. He suspected it was a mighty interesting place—though fairly noisy.

After a moment she added in a different tone, "At least I'm trying, Andy. I noticed what Dodie wore today, too—her blue seersucker suit. I'm practicing *really looking*." She caught his glance and held it. "Seems to me *you* should start practicing believing things."

Andy, remembering the White Queen, smiled in spite of himself. "Like six impossible things before breakfast?"

"Why not?" asked Kat.

He didn't answer, but he didn't challenge the question. It was beginning to seem an inevitable next step in this hind-side-to, *Through the Looking Glass* situation. He was forced to admit he already believed *some* things he couldn't see or touch. Gases, radio waves, burnt-out stars. But only a *few*.

He stood up abruptly. "Are there any more of those doughnuts?"

"You can have the rest of mine. Andy, what about the graveyard? Shouldn't we just go *look*, before I have to go up and do Czerny?"

"Not right now, I haven't finished the trail," Andy mumbled. "Maybe this evening . . ."

But by evening, as he had more or less counted on, they were all busy with the artists, and over the weekend the routine details of running the Lodge crowded everything else into the background. Eighteen art students—who turned out to be mostly post-middle-aged ladies with decided ideas about comfort—was a lot of guests for just a summer staff to cope with; Andy was drafted for busboy duties, and kept being called on to show somebody where the creek was, or find an old blanket, or hunt up another folding chair. Kat took over mid-afternoon coffee and the salads for dinner. Their regular chores had to be worked in. They couldn't even think about their own affairs until so late that they were both out of steam.

"Tell you what," Andy said as they let themselves into the cottage at eight o'clock Sunday evening and fell with one accord into the nearest chairs. "Let's just sit right here until bedtime. Tomorrow morning they'll all go away."

"Yeah, even Dodie, remember?" After a minute Kat added, "I *had* been thinking we could have a driving lesson—maybe tomorrow afternoon. But—"

She looked a doubtful question at Andy; he could only shrug. Personally he felt funny about going back to the Buckles', at least for a while. Especially to ask a favor.

Kat read him correctly. "Well, anyway, we'll have lots of free time while Dodie's gone. For driving lessons—or whatever."

Sure, thought Andy. He sighed and quit fighting it. Whatever.

Right after breakfast Monday morning Dodie headed for Portland and the house reroofing, remarking that at least she didn't have to do it herself. Fifteen minutes later the twins were on their way down the wooded hillside—ostensibly because Kat wanted another duck-egg omelet for dinner.

"Though we might not have to go clear down to the poultry house," she added innocently. "I mean if Ellerton happened to be working in the cemetery, well, I mean—"

Andy just said, "I know what you mean."

By unspoken agreement they walked on past the weed-grown cemetery corner and stood for a moment staring up toward Beaver Rock. Nobody there, of course. Just a dark, crouching boulder, old as the hills it was part of. It did look a little like a beaver, mused Andy—anyway more than like a dog. It also looked terminally deserted and lonesome as time.

"No use waiting, Andy," Kat said softly. "It's our move. Come on."

Without comment Andy followed her back to the iron fence and along the grassy track in front of it. There was no sign of Ellerton, and the tall gates were closed. But—as Kat immediately discovered—they were not locked.

Andy stepped in front of her, pushed them open, and went in.

Almost at once he found himself wondering why he'd been dreading it all this time—just what he'd imagined would happen when he walked onto this special ground. From outside, the tangle of blackberry had made the place look as forbidding as the Sleeping Beauty's bramble-entwined palace—and the longer he'd stayed outside, the more hostile it had seemed. But from inside, thanks to Ellerton's labors, it was merely a green and peaceful half acre, broken by an occasional lilac clump, sprinkled with wildflowers, and studded with weathered and tilted stones.

An old oak tree grew near the center; in its shade a rectangle traced by a crumbling boundary of marble held a whole family of Harpers—ten graves, ranging from Josiah Edwin and his Beloved Wife Abigail Martha down through a half dozen grown-up offspring to Effie, aged three years—and "Baby," who apparently died before there was time to name him or her. Beyond the oak tree was a similar cluster of Coreys, including one age-blackened stone bearing two names, both "infants," and the inscription, "Thy will be done." And there were older children: an Alexander Jenkins, born 1851, died 1862, and an Elizabeth Jane Darnell, whose tender age, "13 years, 7 months, 1 day," sorrowfully carved in granite, had outlasted her by a hundred years. But many more stones testified to rugged pioneer constitutions—Harpers, Coreys, Bakers, Clarks, who had lived out their threescore ten. A few had done better, including an extremely durable Sweet born in 1802 who had unquestionably come west in a covered wagon to survive until 1899. And one Walter Huddleston, perhaps born on the trail in 1848, was still around in 1940.

Andy was beginning to enjoy himself, just as he'd thought he might that day he'd first rattled past here in the wagon with the 4-H'ers and wondered about old dates on the graves.

Then Kat called, "Andy! I've found a lot of Sweets."

She had wandered off toward the far side of the fence, where the gentle downward slope of the enclosure changed to the steeper one of the hay field. She was now prowling around the rearmost corner. It was rampantly overgrown, blackberry mingling with wild rose vines and a fringe of tall grasses; obviously Ellerton had not got around there yet this season. Andy crossed toward her over ground so knotted and bunched with its exuberant growth of clover that it was like walking on a lumpy mattress. Kat was moving eagerly from stone to stone, bent almost double in an effort to read the weathered and blackened inscriptions.

"Mary Sweet . . . Samuel Sweet . . . Elijah L. . . . Sarah . . . is that *Jacob*? Andy, I think I've found— oh, no, that's *Jonas*. Anyhow, it's a—a grown-up. Look—over there. Can you read that one?"

"Martha," supplied Andy. He began to move along the next row. "Ellen Lulu, aged two years. Henry. Donald Arthur. Matthew. Ruby . . ." He broke off, and stood silent before an odd little stone, shaped like a column with a peaked top, which stood a little apart, near the fence, almost under the brambles. After a moment he made him-self reach out and lift aside a thorny runner.

"Jacob Samuel Sweet," read the worn inscription. "*Apr. 16, 1867–Feb. 4, 1876. R.I.P. Beloved child.*"

Beloved child. Not quite ten years old. Doubtless towheaded, with sky-blue eyes and a husky voice.

So there it was.

Andy backed up a couple of steps, bumped into a gravestone, and without planning to, sat down on it. Once there, he stayed. He felt he might never get up again. Kat ran to him, stumbling over the clover tufts, and went still and silent in her turn before the little column.

After a long time, Andy said calmly—though it came out sounding as though his tonsils needed oil —"Remember, it doesn't prove a thing."

"No," Kat agreed. After another long time she added, "Only . . . Andy?"

"What?"

Kat took a deep, uneven breath and turned to face him. "If it doesn't, how come we knew what name to look for on the grave?"

CHAPTER TEN

It was only one of the questions Andy couldn't answer—unless he was prepared to accept the boy of the hillside as the ghost of the little boy in the grave. Even if he did accept it, questions remained, which he was willing to bet Kat couldn't answer either. He told her so, after they'd left the graveyard, closed the iron gates carefully behind them, and gone to sit on a rail of the pasture fence.

"Like what?" she demanded.

"Like why pick on us to solve his problem—a couple of strangers? Why not his own family? You can't throw a rock around here without hitting somebody named Sweet. Or at least a close neighbor—one of those Coreys or Harpers or Clarks or—"

"Maybe he's tried them all!" Kat countered. "Maybe they couldn't see him—the way I couldn't at first. Or maybe they didn't believe in him. The way *you* didn't at first."

"Maybe I still don't," Andy retorted. "What kind of honest-to-goodness self-respecting ghost would come haunting around in the middle of the afternoon? That's a dumb time of day for spooks—

and it's when I've usually seen him—about two or three o'clock. And another thing: Why would a *little kid* ghost come back just because a *bed's* been stolen? Kids don't care about furniture. And they can sleep anywhere."

"But it was *his* bed, Andy. Anyway," Kat said thoughtfully, "I'll bet we could find that out."

"How?"

"Ask the Sweets. Dawnelle—and J.B. *You* know. About the heirloom bed."

"Oh, yeah. The one with the rubies and diamonds in the bedpost. And carted across the prairie in a wagon train. Didn't you see the dates on that stone? The Jacob Sweet in that grave wasn't even born till after the Civil War. Weren't any more wagon trains by then."

"That doesn't matter," Kat said patiently. "It could've already been an heirloom when he *was* born. In fact, it would make him all the more—"

"Oh, Kat, give up." Andy sighed, propped his elbows on his knees, and thrust all his fingers into his hair. *Beloved child.* He wished he could forget that.

"What were the dates?" Kat asked after a moment, adding guiltily, "I guess I didn't *really look* at the inscription."

Andy recited it for her, wishing he'd never seen it.

"Oh, yeah, I remember. What does 'R.I.P.' mean?"

"Rest In Peace. I think they used to put that on lots of stones."

There was a rather dismal silence, which Kat broke. "It's so pathetic! To think that poor little boy might've been trying for—for a hundred years, Andy!—to get somebody to find that bed."

"But *what* bed? That's the problem." Once more, Andy went over their only information: *Somebody stole my bed. I don't have any place to sleep.* For a hundred years—maybe longer. "He's sure not Resting In Peace, poor kid," he sighed as he prepared to heave himself off the fence. "Not resting at all."

At that point something happened in his brain— everything took a sort of half turn and made a new pattern. He went rigid, and found that Kat had done the same and was staring at him.

"Andy," she said.

He was already nodding, leaping to the ground. "Yeah. I finally got there too. His bed! *He means his grave. His grave's his bed!*"

"Why didn't we think of it?" Kat exclaimed as she tumbled after him. "People always call a grave a 'resting place' and death 'eternal sleep' and—and . . . it's so obvious!"

It was obvious. Now that they *had* thought of it,

Andy added to himself. It had been anything but clear before. And it made something else much less clear. "So how could somebody steal it?" he demanded.

That called for another long stare at each other, with only wild conjecture as the result. With one accord they headed swiftly back to the iron gates, pushed them open without ceremony, and stumbled across the cemetery to the grave.

There was the little stone column, the name, the dates, the half-obliterated *Beloved Child* overhung with grasses and trailing vines. It seemed impossible to believe that anybody had been near it—except Ellerton, once a year or so—for the century since little Jacob Sweet had died. They gazed in silence at the undisturbed turf, the bunchy clover. Was he in there, then? Or not? And if not, where was he? And what *was* buried in the grave?

Kat said, "It's time to tell somebody."

Reluctantly, Andy nodded. Part of him longed to tell somebody—somebody older, somebody capable of dealing with such a bucket of eels as this was turning out to be. The other part pulled back in a kind of panic. How on earth to explain? Who would even listen long enough to . . . inevitably, it was Mr. Buckle's face that appeared in his mind, before he could remind himself that things were different now. "We'll tell Dodie," he said abruptly. "I don't know what she can do, but . . ."

"We can't tell Dodie. She's in Portland."

"Oh, yeah." Any postponement was welcome. "Well, we can tell her when she gets back."

"But then she'll be all involved with that Senior group—fifteen old ladies who'll all want three pillows apiece and warm milk at four A.M. Let's tell Mr. Buckle—*now*."

"We told him days ago! Or tried to. And remember how he acted."

"That was because he's seen Jacob himself. I *know* it was. Besides, we know a lot more to tell him now." Kat sighed impatiently as Andy merely shook his head. "Then what about Ellerton? He's the caretaker of this place, after all."

"Aw, no, we hardly know Ellerton! We can't go bothering—"

"Andy, why are you dragging your *feet* so?"

Andy tried to speak and ended up waving his hands and then jamming them into his pockets as he started for the gate, head down. He didn't know why he was suddenly fighting against reason, or why he felt so certain that telling somebody—anybody—all they suspected about Jacob now would shake the foundations of the world. At least, *his* world, the everyday, sensible world where ghosts didn't exist. It was all very well to . . . sort of believe in Jacob privately. But once you open your mouth about a thing like that, you've opened the doors to—well, you just didn't know *what*.

"Andy, stop running away from me!" Kat caught up, just outside the fence, and faced him indignantly. "What's the matter with you? Here we've finally figured out the problem—"

"We haven't! We've figured out what that *bed* is—or think we have. But what about this 'somebody stole it'? How can you steal a grave?"

They looked at each other, the question hanging there between them, the answer growing more and more obvious. Kat finally voiced it, rather shakily.

"You could—dig up what was there and—put in something else instead. And—and—just throw the first thing away somewhere. Or hide it. Or—" She swallowed.

"Or destroy it," Andy finished slowly. "So that nobody could ever find it no matter what they did." He took a deep breath. "No telling what we're getting into."

"We're getting into—opening a grave?" Kat said.

Andy fought down panic. "No chance! That takes real reasons. A little *ghost* told us? Nobody'd even listen."

"Mr. Buckle would." Kat paused, pinning Andy with a look that reminded him forcibly of Dodie. "We've got to try—for Jacob's sake. Andy, just think about Jacob a minute!"

"All right, all right!" exploded Andy, who had been trying hard *not* to think about Jacob. He seized the least of two impossibilities. "We'll go talk to Ellerton."

But the moment they reached the lane they saw Mr. Buckle—sitting in a two-wheeled cart blocking the way just ahead, directly opposite Beaver Rock. His back was to them, his head turned toward the rock, his elbows on his knees as if he had been there for some time. The big Belgian hitched to the cart—a light-colored mare they hadn't seen before—had begun to stamp and bob her head with impatience.

For an instant Andy knew a wild hope that Jacob might be there too, helping out for once by telling the whole story himself. The hope died as Mr. Buckle glanced over his shoulder at the sound of their footsteps. His face showed only puzzled conjecture. As they walked toward him, he smiled wryly and made no effort to pretend he was merely resting his already restless horse. Just the way he was sitting there looking at them, his gaze direct and candid as ever, untied some kind of hard knot inside Andy.

"Hello, twins," he said. "Glad you happened along. I've missed you."

"We've missed you, too!" Kat blurted.

"Good. I was scared you might be kinda peeved at me. But I was just about to go phone you for a conference." He jerked his head toward the rock. "About all this."

Andy's last doubt vanished. Nobody was going to have to pretend anything. "Was he up there?" he asked. "I mean just now?"

"Nope. Not just now, or any of the other times in the last few days when I've strolled up here and waited. Of course—no reason he should be, specially. Any number of reasons why he might be home, or gone fishing, or wherever he . . ." Mr. Buckle let the rest trail off in a baffled sigh.

"You *have* seen him, then? Our Jacob?" Kat asked.

"I've got a hunch I've been seeing him off and on for a good long time. Never struck me till the other day, when I heard myself saying I'd known a kid like that by sight for years. I tell you, I felt like one of these Belgians had kicked me. How in Sam Hill could I have been seeing the same little nine-year-old for *years*? He'd be nineteen or twenty by this time. I just never stopped to think of it before."

"But you told us it probably wasn't the same boy," Andy reminded him.

"Oh, I know I did. And maybe it isn't, maybe it isn't. Then I went on and said they all look alike at that age, and *that's* a damfool remark. They all look like nobody but themselves, at any age. Especially this kid, somehow or other."

"*Yeah!*" Kat and Andy agreed in chorus.

Mr. Buckle glanced again at the empty hillside, then back to the twins, raising his heavy eyebrows. "Something mighty peculiar here. Been riding me."

"Us too!" Andy said with feeling.

"You want to talk it over?"

"We were just on our way to . . ." Andy stopped there. No need to mention Ellerton. It was all right now to tell Mr. Buckle instead. The thing inside him that had been feeling like a dried-up prune was expanding to its usual size, and the relief was so great he was almost afraid to trust it. *He hasn't heard everything yet,* he cautioned himself.

Mr. Buckle nodded. "Sorry I only got a one-seat rig here. I'll drive on down, turn Goldie out with the others. How about you meet me in the tack room?"

Gladly they followed him down the lane, light-footed and almost light-headed with the comfort of knowing they were no longer alone with their puzzle.

He came into the barn shortly after them, carrying the cart harness, and reached down a can of saddle soap and a rag. "Now tell me again," he commanded as he settled on his stool.

Andy braced himself and launched into the complete tale of Jacob and the bed, considerably hindered by Kat, who kept breaking in to add some decorative detail. Even with decorations it was a brief story—five sightings, dozens of questions asked and unasked, no answers.

So much was easy. The rest, today's part of the story, had him stammering right away. "And we kept wondering—about this bed. What he *meant*. We couldn't figure it out. It seemed so—"

"Andy, I'll do it," said Kat. She faced Mr. Buckle. "Today we did figure it out—we think. There's a—a grave—up in the—old graveyard, and it—and it—" Kat gasped and bit her lip.

"You found a grave for a *child* named Jacob Sweet?" Mr. Buckle was no longer saddle soaping the harness, only listening intently.

"Yeah, we did," Andy told him, feeling as if the words were being extracted like a tooth. "Eighteen sixty-seven to eighteen seventy-six. Whoever's buried there was nine years old." He swallowed. "Mr. Buckle, I don't believe in ghosts! I—"

"Do you?" Kat put in quickly.

They both waited without breathing. Mr. Buckle gazed into the air between them, chewing his lip thoughtfully, apparently chewing the question, too. "I dunno," he said at last. "Not the kind in sheets. But go ahead—finish."

"Well—that's about all. But we—we thought if that Jacob Sweet was our Jacob—"

Mr. Buckle's gaze was fully comprehending. "All right, I get the picture. . . . A ghost of retribution, eh?" he murmured as if to himself. "Trying all this time—more than a hundred years, by golly—to get justice done."

"Maybe only to get his own bed back," Kat said softly.

There was still that one final thing to be hauled out into the open, and Andy hauled it. "The question is, who *is* in his bed—or what—and how do we find out?"

"That's not one question, that's three—all of them whopperoos," said Mr. Buckle. He went back to his harness soaping, and for a few moments worked unhurriedly, as if there were nobody there but him. Then he added, "And they all need to be answered, one way or another. In my opinion."

Kat said eagerly, "Then you think we ought to—"

"Wait, wait, whoa. So far I only just—get the picture. As for figuring what we ought to do—" Mr. Buckle pulled in a deep breath and blew it out as he stood up, abandoning harness and rag on the workbench. "How can a man begin thinking about something like this? I can't even believe we're talking about it."

"That's how *I* feel!" Andy told him.

"Well, I don't know about you two, but I need some coffee to get started. Come on in the house." As Andy hesitated, Mr. Buckle added with his usual intuitiveness, "Nobody there. Myra's in Harper's Mill—be gone all day. Helping the P.T.A. to can bush beans for the school cafeteria. Never saw the like of the gardens this year—ever'body got beans coming out of their ears. You two like coffee, or would you rather have milk?"

He settled them at the kitchen table with glasses of milk and thick slabs of homemade bread spread with the strawberry jam they had seen Mrs. Buckle starting a couple of weeks before. Then he poured himself a mug full of potent-looking coffee from a speckled enamel pot on the stove and joined them.

"We better line this out pretty firm for ourselves," he began. "Sorta back off and squint at it. First thing is: Can we trust what we were seeing?"

"We all three saw him," Kat pointed out. "At separate times, too. Besides, Andy and I *heard* him."

"That's right, you did," mused Mr. Buckle. "Now, he never said boo to me." He took a thoughtful sip of coffee. "I maybe never gave him the chance. Always just kinda tipped my hat"—he sketched the familiar little half-salute—"and went on by. Wish I hadn't, now, but I just thought he was one of the local kids I didn't know."

He sounded troubled about this, and Andy said, "I thought that, too. But when I found out Kat couldn't see him at all—"

"Yep, that sure would've jogged your elbow. All right, let's say we believe what we saw and heard. Let's go whole hog and say—just to state the case for the believers—that we're certain-sure some little ghost was ousted from his rightful place a hundred-odd years ago and wants it back. Where are we now?"

"I guess the believers would say—duty bound to help him get it," Andy answered.

"Then I'm a believer," Kat said earnestly.

"But Kat!" Andy protested. "Think what it'd mean! Digging up a grave! Mr. Buckle, they'd never let us do that, would they? I mean—imagine explaining this to some—some—judge or some-body! Because wouldn't we have to get—I don't know—a lawyer, or—?"

"I'm not sure what the drill would be," Mr. Buckle said thoughtfully. "Never came up before, in my experience. Tell you the truth, it's kinda unusual in anybody's experience."

"All *my* experience tells me I'm a nonbeliever!" Andy muttered. "But I—I saw Jacob. We talked."

"Yeah, well, for that matter 'experience' can mean almost anything. Maybe this is just a new kind. A kind most folks never run into." Mr. Buckle grinned briefly. "Don't know whether to feel flattered or discriminated against."

The little joke relaxed all three of them. Kat laughed outright, and even Andy smiled and felt some knots untie. No use getting all uptight, he told himself. Won't help a bit. "There's other things seem just as impossible, once you think about 'em," he admitted. He explained Kat's idea about the old burnt-out stars.

Mr. Buckle gave her an interested look and remarked that there seemed to be a good bit under
her hat besides a lot of pretty red hair. Then he
said, "We haven't stated the case for the non-
believers yet—but we hardly need to. General
public's going to rear right up on its hind legs the
minute we mention opening a grave."

"That's what I can't stand to think about—the
general public," Andy muttered—by which they
both, he knew, meant Harper's Mill. He could
actually feel the gooseflesh rise. "Look how they
took on about those eggs!"

Kat said scornfully, "You mean, 'What Will
People Say?' I'm not going to let that stop me!"

"You aren't going to be let *start*, even, while
everybody's yelling and screaming," Andy retorted.

"True," said Mr. Buckle. "And I've got to say
that to a certain extent I'm on the side of the yellers
and screamers. I wouldn't want to be a party to
opening a grave without something more to go on
than a sort of theory." He finished his coffee and
set the mug down with an emphatic thump. "We're
going to have to find some real evidence. Some
hard, convincing facts."

"I know one," Kat said promptly. She threw a
quelling glance at Andy. "And you couldn't explain it either! We knew whose grave to look for.

We knew Jacob's name. And we'd never been in that graveyard in our lives."

Mr. Buckle studied her with a little pucker between his eyebrows—obviously trying to explain it himself. But after a moment he nodded and said, "Point one for the believers. If we can get folks to believe *you*."

"They'd think we were *lying?*" Kat gasped.

"They'd think you were maybe fooling yourselves," Mr. Buckle said gently. "Playing a made-up game that got away from you. It's been done. Ever study in school about the Salem witch trials?"

"Oh, yeah!" said Andy, enlightened. "Some of those old women they hanged really believed, themselves, that they were witches! They must've wanted to be."

"Well, I can see the notion might be fairly attractive—if you were old and nobody liked you and kids threw things at you in the street."

"And murdered your cat," Andy added. Then, as Kat turned to him with a horrified "*Oh!*" he said hastily, "That's probably only rumor," and hurried to get the meeting back on track. "What I'd like to find are some good, hard facts to explain all this some other way. Some kind of *common-sense* way. Then we wouldn't have to go public or worry about graves or lawyers or *any* of that stuff. I'd like to prove it never happened!"

"That's just being an ostrich," Kat informed him. "It *did* happen."

"On the other hand, trying to prove it didn't is as good a way to tackle the thing as trying to prove it did," said Mr. Buckle. He stood up, picked up the empty milk glasses between two thick fingers and carried them and his mug to the sink. "Suppose we work both sides of the road the next few days—see what we come up with, evidence for or against. Open minds, that's what we need."

"And ideas about where to start." Andy sighed as he and Kat followed with their plates.

CHAPTER ELEVEN

"Where we start," Kat said thoughtfully a couple of hours later, "is with the Sweet family."

They had been back to the Lodge to touch base with Mrs. Corey and Mrs. Sweet, who with a couple of teenage nieces were getting the place ready for the next onslaught. Afterwards, having augmented Mr. Buckle's bread and jam with a lunch of potato chips and pop, they had wandered back down the hill like water seeking its own level, hoping for inspiration. They stood now in the far corner of the old graveyard, gazing once more at the enigmatic little stone column with its worn inscription.

"The Sweet family?" repeated Andy. There were Sweets all around them here, presumably sleeping peacefully under their tilted old stones. He waved an all-inclusive gesture. "Go right ahead, if you think you can get any answers."

"I mean the live ones," Kat told him patiently. "As you very well know." They walked back over the lumpy mattress of clover and out to their

perches on the pasture fence. "Like J.B. and Dawnelle."

Andy considered this, feeling his usual dreading
reluctance. "They couldn't tell us anything. The
only Jacob Sweet they know is their uncle in Portland. Anyhow—I don't want to go spreading it
around!"

"We don't need to mention anything about
Jacob. Just sort of—ask things. There could be old
family stories, something that would give us a
clue. We could even ask about that bed."

Andy stared at her. "The one with the jewels in
the bedpost? But we *know* about the bed now."

"Yes—but what if we're just playing a game
that's got away from us?"

Andy blinked. "Have you and I changed sides?"

"No. But I'm keeping an open mind. Mr.
Buckle said hunt up evidence for or against, didn't
he? Then prove or disprove—it's all the same.
Well, you do one, and I'll do the other. But we need
evidence to work on. So far we've got one point
for: We knew Jacob's name."

"I doubt if we've even got that," said Andy, who
had been giving the matter some thought. With
rather gloomy satisfaction he shared his conclusions. "Suppose somebody *else* has been playing a
game—a big fat joke on us? Found some little kid
to stand out there by the rock and act mysterious,

so we'd get all worked up and finally locate that grave, and charge around making fools of ourselves, just the way we've been doing!"

Kat had gone pale with dismay. "But Andy! Who'd do that to us? So *mean!*"

"I dunno. One of those Harper's Mill kids—just because we're new—or city kids or something. It might not have seemed mean at first, you know, just—funny."

"It's *not* funny! It's *awful!*" Kat's eyes had got suspiciously bright. Next instant the skies cleared as she added, "It's not true, either."

"I didn't say it was *true*—I only said—"

"Because how could a joke explain *Mr. Buckle* seeing Jacob around for years and years? Or me not seeing him at all until I tried and tried and . . . "

"I don't know." Or the look on Jacob's face, Andy thought—that light bulb that came on when I said I'd find his bed. If that was some ordinary kid putting on an act, he ought to be on TV. "But something's got to explain it! I was just trying to find some plain, ordinary reason—"

Kat snapped, "It's not a time to plod along looking for plain, ordinary reasons! It's a time to use our brains—supposing we've got any."

"*Okay.*" Andy threw his hands up. "You use yours, Madame Sherlock Holmes. I'll *plod* along and do just what you say."

"Then I say we go find out if Dawnelle and J.B. have ever heard anything about a missing valuable bed."

Andy slid off the rail to the ground and stood waiting.

"Oh," said Kat. "Right now?"

"No use stalling around. If we've finally thought up something to do, let's *do* it. I'll even go see old spooky Aunt Henry if you want."

Kat climbed down the rails and they started for the Sweets' lane and the Christmas tree farm.

This time, when they approached the old white house with its backdrop of juniper and holly, they avoided the front door and went around to the sagging screened porch at the rear. A huge cork elm shaded half of the backyard; from the circle of sparse grass beneath it a small golden-brown dog sprang up, barking hysterically and backing away from them. Seeing that it was going to end up cornered in an angle of the house, Andy stopped, hunkered down to the dog's level, and began telling it what a good, fierce, scary watchdog it was. The dog's ears went flat at once, and its tongue came out in an embarrassed smile. By the time Dawnelle appeared at the screen door, wiping her hands on a very work-worn apron, the dog was sidling closer to Andy, plumy tail making an occasional sweep, ears going uncertainly up and down.

"It's okay, Brownie," Dawnelle said, sounding

a little embarrassed herself, and stripping off the apron to throw it out of sight. "He's an awful coward," she added to the twins.

Andy said, "Aw, he's a good dog, aren't you, Brownie?"

But Kat, after hesitating a moment, blurted, "I know how he feels. I'm a coward too, sometimes."

Dawnelle's slow, shy smile began as she came down the weathered back steps, and walked across the grass toward them. "You're talking about those Belgians."

"I—yeah, I was sort of scared of them. I mean, just at first."

"Well, don't feel bad. Half of us were scared pea green first time we drove."

"Really?" Kat's shoulders relaxed a bit.

"Honest. *I* sure was."

"But somebody—laughed at me."

"Sue Harper." Dawnelle rolled her turquoise eyes, disposing once and for all of Sue Harper, and this time Kat smiled, too.

Andy, who by now was sealing a fast friendship with Brownie by massaging behind his silky ears, decided that it wasn't going to take six months for those two after all—or even six more days. He stood up and cleared his throat, looking meaningfully at Kat. This was her project; he was just tagging—*plodding*—along behind.

Kat got the message and acknowledged it by

turning firmly back to Dawnelle, "We came to ask you something. You and J.B. both."

"Okay." Dawnelle looked curious and interested. "I think he's upstairs changing—just got back from Sugar Meadows. Lemme holler at him."

As she started toward the house, J.B. himself came out, stocking-footed, said "Oh, hi!" to the twins, picked up a pair of very grubby workshoes waiting just outside the door and sat down on the top step to put them on. "Ever find your Jacob Sweet?" he asked Andy.

It was not a question Andy was prepared to answer. Anyway, if he said "No," Kat was sure to be saying "Yes" at the very same minute. With a warning glance at her, he said, "We kind of gave that up. But we were wondering—I mean, this is an awful stupid question, but—"

"It's not," Kat said crisply. "We've got interested in—in local history. We saw a lot of Sweets in the old graveyard up there. We figured they must've been pioneers."

Smart, thought Andy, giving her an admiring look. He would never have thought of that approach himself.

J.B., tying his shoes, said, "Oh, yeah, this farm's part of the original land claim—quite a bit of it's still in the family. Dad's cousin Charlie Sweet, he owns the piece just north of here, and Uncle Millard still has about fifteen acres down toward town. 'Course a lot of the Sweet land was sold off."

"Or went for debt," Dawnelle put in, exchanging a glance with him.

"Yeah—my grandpa's brother—he was a no-goodnik," J.B. said with a rueful grin. He stood up, scraped dried mud off his right shoe on the edge of the step. "But there was six hundred forty acres to begin with. Old Samuel Sweet claimed it in 1847—him and his wife and six kids. Came out in a wagon train from Kentucky or somewhere."

"Pennsylvania," Dawnelle said.

Kat wet her lips and swallowed. "I s'pose they —brought along everything they owned—I mean, furniture and stuff?"

"Well, they started out with it," J.B. said. "I don't think much of it got here. I guess you could follow that Oregon trail from about Wyoming on just by spotting people's big grandfather clocks and four-posters and stuff thrown out on the prairie. Oxen started giving out, and they just had to lighten the loads."

"Four-posters." Kat pounced on the operative word. "We—heard somewhere there was a valu-able—piece of furniture in your family. Sort of an antique bed, or something? You know anything about that?"

The two Sweets regarded her in mystified silence, and shook their heads. J.B. said, "Far as I know, our family never owned anything valuable except our land."

Kat darted a glance of appeal at Andy, who pitched in. "Maybe somebody else might know? Your grandma, maybe?"

"She's dead," Dawnelle told him. "So's grand-daddy—long ago. We could ask Dad."

J.B. laughed suddenly and said, "Or Aunt Henry."

Kat pounced again, but so smoothly that nobody but Andy would have known it for a pounce. "Oh, I've heard about her! Is she a real old lady—with lots of cats, and—"

"And crazy as a bedbug," added J.B., picking up a pair of work gloves from the ledge of the porch.

"She's not either!" retorted Dawnelle, though she went a little pink. "She's just—kind of differ-ent. Where'd you hear about her?" she asked Kat.

"From Mrs. Corey—the one who cooks at the Lodge." Kat's voice was innocent as a two-year-old's. "I just happened to be asking about ghosts, and she said I ought to talk to—"

"Ghosts?" J.B. interrupted. He had been edging away, pulling on a glove, obviously about to excuse himself from the conversation, but he halted abruptly. His black-lashed blue eyes narrowed in amusement as he stared at Kat. "Sounds to me as if you've already met Aunt Henry!"

"What makes you think so?" Andy asked him.

"I put two and two together, is all. You *just happened* to be asking about ghosts. And you just happened to ask *us* about a *bed!* Well—it's her favorite story!"

"Then there *has* been a ghost around here?" Kat dropped all pretense of keeping cool. "I mean for a long time? A kind of regular ghost, that people keep seeing and—"

"Aw, no-o-o." J.B. was laughing in an embarrassed way—rather as if he were embarrassed for Kat. "It's just a story. Listen, Aunt Henry is really kind of—well, she's real *old*. I think ninety-five. She makes up things."

"Not always," Dawnelle said suddenly.

"Well, mostly."

Andy said, "What is the story?"

J.B. turned to him, shrugged apologetically. "Oh, the way *she* tells it, there's some kind of ghost around here and he was a Sweet when he was alive. And he says something about a lost bed."

"Lost? Or stolen?" Kat said swiftly.

"*I* dunno. She's never seen this—whatever-it-is —herself—she admits it. Probably nobody ever has. It's nothing but one of those old yarns. Something big kids tease little kids with—just to scare 'em, you know."

He grinned sheepishly at Dawnelle, who said, "*Yeah*. I know." She looked hard at Kat. "You want to talk to Aunt Henry? I'll take you up there if you want."

Andy began a protest but Kat drowned him out. "Yes! I want to know more about it."

"Just for the historical interest," Andy put in to save face, after a glance at J.B.'s, which expressed the sort of kindly tolerance one gives a three-year-old's account of the bear in his closet.

However, all J.B. said was, "She'll tell you a lot of history, all right. But take it with a teaspoon of salt." To Dawnelle he added, "If you want to go right now, I'll haul all three of you on my way to the canyon. That's if you don't mind riding with the garbage."

"It's in sacks," Dawnelle said quickly, after a glance at Kat's startled face. "Dad's got his compost pile up there—for the garden, you know."

"Oh, yeah," said Kat, who obviously didn't know but just as obviously was willing to go wherever Dawnelle took her.

"It's *my* compost pile, if you want the truth of it," J.B. grumbled to Andy as they started toward the barn. "At least I get to do all the hauling and shoveling. Okay, Brownie! Come on, boy, you can go too."

With Brownie frisking and panting and running little ecstatic circles around them, they crossed the big tire-tracked turning space, J.B. splitting off to the barn, the others walking around to the side, where a box trailer, already loaded with an accumulation of prunings and branches and grass clippings and dead pea vines, stood waiting. Brownie took a flying leap and scrambled to the very top, where he sat down regally and waved his tail. By the time the others had climbed up to dispose themselves here and there upon the pile—there were only two small plastic bags of garbage—the tractor had roared to life in the barn. In a moment J.B. came driving it around the corner of the building and backed it up to the trailer. Andy jumped down again to help with the hitch. Then, acting on J.B.'s shouted invitation, he rode standing on the tractor's iron step, hanging on to the seat. They headed back through the fruit orchard behind the barn, bouncing along the grassy aisles between pear trees and apples, walnuts and gnarled old Italian prunes, each tree laden with small green fruit just visible among the leaves.

"I guess none of that'll be ripe till fall," shouted Andy with regret into J.B.'s ear, thinking of all the windfalls going to birds and yellowjackets while he sat in school in Portland.

"Early apples will. Gravensteins in August. Transparents before that—and prunes—you'll get some!" J.B. shouted back with a grin. "Hang on, the next stretch is rough."

The tractor pulling its mixed load was bumping through a stand of tall hollies now, and soon turned

up a wide track between plantings of young firs,
again heading away from the road and deeper into
Sweet property. To Andy, the place still seemed
at least as large as 640 acres, but J.B. hooted with
mirth at the suggestion.

"It's about fifty, all told! You must not have
much idea of the size of an acre."

Andy guessed he hadn't. Until he'd come here
this summer he'd had no idea of the size of a Belgian, either, or the sound of guinea hens or the
taste of a duck egg—or what a satisfaction it was
to get a rocky, rooty, salal-choked trail all cleared
and smooth so that a person could sit there and
listen to the creek and see what birds lived around
those parts.

He'd always been glad Portland was big and
various enough to have a "city" feel. He'd felt
himself a city boy. Now he wondered. There might
be a country boy underneath.

CHAPTER TWELVE

Aunt Henry's house, nestled close beside Hidden Creek where it wound through the Sweet property, a couple of miles below the Lodge, at first looked like part of the landscape—just another tangle of the wild alder and hazel and vine maple and long grasses that grew around the rim of the cultivated land wherever the firs didn't. On closer inspection, when J.B. halted the tractor to let them off, Andy saw a very small house back in the tangle, an odd one that seemed made of bits and pieces of several others.

"It's the old Sweet house," Dawnelle explained as the tractor moved noisily away—Brownie still king of his mountain—and the three of them picked their way along a twisting, grass-fringed path that looked as if it had been made by deer or foxes—as perhaps it had. "The first house built on the claim. I think it used to be all logs. But it's been patched up and added to and half fallen down so often it's just kind of a mess by now. Here, around this way."

The twins followed her around the corner of the house to a low, sagging porch fronting the creek. Two marmalade cats and a gray one sprang from the step and fled as they approached. A black-and-white one slid into the bushes.

"Auntie?" Dawnelle called. "Auntie, it's me, can we come in?"

"It's who?" came a thin, querulous old voice from somewhere inside. "Oh, *Dawnie*! My lands yes, come on in, child, no need to ask. . . . Who's that with you?"

"It's Andy and Kat Peterson. They're my new friends from up at the Lodge," Dawnelle said in a tone of simple pride that made Kat turn pink under her freckles and surprised Andy into stumbling over the doorstep. She makes us sound like an *A* in math, he thought, feeling as if she had suddenly given him a present. It hadn't occurred to him that local kids might have been wanting to know *them*, too.

He followed the two girls into a room so low-ceilinged he instinctively ducked his head, across a floor that made him feel like a sailor on a rolling deck. It was less like a room than like a sort of untidy nest—a pack-rat's nest, maybe, or a magpie's. The only usable space was right in the middle, and three big, shabby, comfortable chairs occupied that. The rest of the room merely provided storage for old chests of drawers and bookcases stuffed not only with books but everything from cardboard boxes to pieced quilts. Little paths led through the furniture to a kitchen and a dim tiny bedroom, with somewhere, no doubt, an even tinier bath. There was a pervading smell of age and peppermints and cats.

The latter were much in evidence—a calico and an outsize tabby dozed together on a shelf, a white one was just vanishing through a doorway as they came in, and a silken black with topaz eyes lounged on Aunt Henry's lap and alternately blinked and glared at them.

Aunt Henry, a scrap of a little old lady occupying about half of her faded armchair, seemed as much a piece of her house as the house seemed a piece of the landscape. She had dandelion-fluff white hair and sharp black eyes, and made even Kat look strapping. She put out a hand that seemed all veins and fragile bones, clutched Andy's with startling strength and said, "My! *You're* a big 'un!"

He grinned, and a good deal to his own surprise retorted, "And you're a *little* 'un." For some reason he felt instantly at home with her, as if he had known her for years.

She gave a high screech of a laugh and shoved him toward a chair, then pulled Kat toward her. "Here. Sit on the arm of my chair here, so you can pet Devil. He looks the part—don't he, now? But it's all show, he's a lazy good-for-nothing old kitty and the tamest one I got. Dawnie, what you up to?"

"I want you to tell Kat and Andy about the Sweet ghost, Auntie. They're interested in history. Pioneers, and all."

"The Sweet ghost . . . Ohhh—" The old lady's eyes opened wider and seemed even blacker as she rolled them toward one then another of her visitors. "That's old Sam'l Sweet hisself, that is. You oughta come up here sometime in the late evenin', set here with me with the lights off—you'd see 'im. I have. Lotsa times. He don't mind my livin' in his house, but he checks up on me. Don't want me to move things around too much, or—"

"Auntie, that's not the ghost I mean. The other one—you know—about the bed."

"Oh, the *little* fella!" Aunt Henry exclaimed, and Andy felt the hairs lift on the back of his neck. He shot a glance at Kat, and caught her in the act of shooting one at him. "Yes, that one's just a young'un," Aunt Henry went on dreamily. "So I'm told. Never saw 'im myself. But my aunt Anna Harper—her that was Sweet afore she married— she told me he was just a little boy."

"Did *she* see him?" Kat put in breathlessly.

"Oh, many's the time. Many and many. She knew 'im, y'know—when he was live and walkin' around. Well, he was her brother! My Papa's, too. No use thinkin' to ask *her* about 'im, though." The old woman's voice and eyes both sharpened as she peered up, birdlike, at Kat, perched on the chair arm beside her. "Anna's been dead these forty years. *I'm* the one knows about him now. Only one left."

"He doesn't—show up anymore, then?" Andy asked her.

"Nope. Musta given up. Or found his bed," Aunt Henry added with a sudden cackle of amusement. "They do say he went on about that bed of his. 'Lost my bed,' he'd say. 'Oh-h-h, won't somebody find my bed for me. I got no bed to sleep in.' And then he'd sorta gro-o-oan and si-i-igh, and wa-a-ail like one of them screech owls—y'ever hear a screech owl, honey?" she asked Kat suddenly.

"I—I don't know," Kat faltered.

Andy said, "I have. They sound pretty spooky all right. Till you know what they are. Then they just sound like screech owls." His neck hairs had settled down again. Aunt Henry's little ghost didn't sound much like Jacob. "You ever hear this little ghost's name?" he asked.

"Oh . . . seems like Anna told me. I dunno. It was long years ago." Aunt Henry, sagging deeper in her chair, seemed to fade and dwindle like her voice, and she gazed toward the window as if the rosebush scraping the glass were miles away. "I do think, though," she said, coming abruptly back to life, "there was a little fella died of diphtheria, 'way back. I do think she said that. It was 'fore my time. Musta been way, way back."

"Like—eighteen seventy-six?" ventured Kat.

"Well, that's way back, all right," Aunt Henry said with her little shriek of laughter. She looked dreamily out the window again, stroking the black cat, which woke up and began a vigorous face washing. "Dawnie, gimme that old album," she said as an afterthought.

"We've got a picture?" Dawnelle asked in surprise, "Of the *ghost*?"

"Don't be a fool, girl. Of the young'un died of diphtheria! Go bring it here." Suddenly animated again, she peered up at Kat. "They was diphtheria ever'where when I was young. Oh, all over. Lotsa kids died of it. Never hear of it now, they musta found one of them vaccines. . . . Honey, you remind me of somebody. Now who can that be? You related to the Coreys?"

While Kat was explaining that she was related only to Petersons and Findlays, Andy watched Dawnelle, who had knelt down before one of the old bureaus to rummage in a drawer, and in a moment extracted a bulging black photo album curling with age. "This one, Aunt Henry?" she asked.

"No, no, the *old* one. With the coffee stain on it." To Kat, she went on, "Findlay! That'd be where you get that rusty red Irish hair. I had a Findlay in love with me once—oh, they were all in love with me then, I was a beauty in my day. I coulda married a prince! I tell you true. A prince from Romania come to call on me one day, right here in this room. . . . It was him spilled the coffee on that album. Yes, that's the one, Dawnie. Bring it here."

"A prince!" Kat was obviously entranced. "How come you didn't marry him?"

"Didn't like him. Man who can't hang on to his coffee cup. I didn't marry any of 'em," Aunt Henry said scornfully. She pushed Devil off her lap and opened the album.

Andy, leaving his chair for a better view of the book, encountered Dawnelle's slow smile, half embarrassed, half defensive. Apparently the Romanian prince was of a piece with old Samuel's landlordish ghost, and should be taken with considerable salt.

They heard a lot about the Sweet family in the next thirty minutes, especially those long-dead members whose stiffly posed, faded likenesses were preserved in the album, along with a view of the actual old sawmill of Harper's Mill, and one of a real stagecoach and a four-horse team. Aunt Henry browsed unhurriedly through the yellowing pages, identifying great-great grandmothers and seventh cousins, untangling bits of family tree, relishing ancient scandals or recounting, with an air of drama, some remarkable event prefaced by "They do say—" which Andy judged usually called for the saltshaker. He had some doubts, for example, that President Teddy Roosevelt had ever pronounced Aunt Henry's biscuits the lightest he'd ever tasted—or that great-great-Uncle Jonas had discovered Yellowstone Park.

But the last page of long ago Sweets was turned without revealing a picture of the little diphtheria victim.

"Auntie, it must be in the black one after all," Dawnelle said as the fragile old hands closed the album.

"What must?" asked Aunt Henry in a threadlike voice. She seemed to come and go like the Lodge lights on a windy night, suddenly dimming and flickering then glowing bright as ever when the current revived. "Oh, yes. Well, I think that was a tintype after all." Her eyes, not sharp and birdlike now but dim with their ninety-odd years, slowly scanned the wall above the bookcases. "Yonder it is. That little oval one. I knew it was somewhere."

All three of them were bumping into each other and into the crowding furniture trying to cross the room. Dawnelle made it first, and took the little oval frame off the wall. It was silver, badly tarnished, and the little metal picture inside was tarnished, too—or worn nearly down to the tin, Andy couldn't tell which. He could barely discern a child —a boy, to judge from the homemade-looking cropped pants and high, buttoned shoes which were the most visible items. He might have been towheaded and his features Jacob's, but it was impossible to say for sure. The image was all but transparent. It was a ghost picture, after all.

Andy met Kat's disappointed glance with one of his own. When he looked back at the picture, Dawnelle had turned it over, and was peering at the dim, spidery writing on the back.

" 'Little Brother Jacob,' " she read slowly. " 'Died of diphtheria, Feb. 4, 1876.' " She turned to Kat. "Didn't you *say* something about 1876? How'd you guess?"

"I didn't guess. I knew," Kat whispered, staring at the inscription.

Andy said quickly, "We noticed a little kid's grave in the old cemetery. Same year. Same name. Kind of interesting to—hitch it up with a real person. Thanks a lot for bringing us up here. Kat, we'd better say goodbye to Aunt Henry and—"

He turned, broke off. Aunt Henry was asleep, looking no more substantial than a faded dress and cardigan thrown over the chair. Devil, back in her lap on top of the album, was nearly asleep too.

"We'll just sneak out," Dawnelle murmured. "She needs her naps."

The two marmalade cats had returned to the

porch, and again leaped for the bushes when they came out, but Andy, looking back from the little twisting fox path, saw them cautiously flowing back, and seized on the change of subject. "They'll be glad to get rid of us," he remarked. "Does she feed 'em all, that little old lady? How does she take care of herself, up there all alone?"

Dawnelle smiled at him over her shoulder. "We take care of her. The cats mostly take care of themselves, there's plenty of field mice. You wanta just start walking back down to the house? J.B.'ll likely be along and pick us up."

By the time they reached the hollies they heard the approaching clamor of the tractor—like a giant clearing his throat—and when it roared alongside they climbed up to join Brownie on the now-empty trailer for the return ride. At the house, they parted —the Sweets heading for their tasks, the twins down the lane.

The moment they were out of earshot Andy said, "D'you think it was him?"

Kat had no need to ask who. "Yes. I know it was hard to tell. . . . But it's *got* to be. Everything *fits*. Even Aunt Henry's story—"

"That didn't fit very well! All that moaning and groaning."

"Well, she made that part up. Or forgot exactly what her Aunt Anna said about it. But it's got to be our Jacob." They crossed the road and started up the Buckles' lane. Kat added, "You sort of—cut me off—when I said I *knew*. You don't think we ought to tell Dawnelle? Even now?"

"No! Not anybody! Until Mr. Buckle says it's time, and it's not anywhere near. We don't know a thing more than we did, not really."

"How can you say that? We know lots more! We know about the diphtheria, we know the—the little buttoned shoes—" Kat's voice quavered.

"Now, don't go getting all sloppy sentimental," Andy ordered, more sharply than he'd intended. For some reason those clumsy small shoes, wrinkled at the ankle where the buttons pulled tightest, had rather got to him, too—maybe because they were the clearest thing in the picture. He couldn't remember whether Jacob-on-the-hillside had been wearing buttoned shoes or none at all. And, he reflected glumly, he'd probably never get another chance to find out; Jacob seemed to have vanished for good, leaving only that big, stupid, dumb rock humping up there like a blank wall where *he* ought to be standing. . . . *I wonder where he goes*, Andy mused, as he had so often when he thought Jacob was just an ordinary boy. He caught himself at it, and this time it gave his ponderings a new direction.

He said suddenly, "Did you get the idea Mr. Buckle always saw Jacob there by the big rock, same place we did?"

He got a minimal answer in barely audible tones; a glance informed him that Kat had retreated into offended hauteur at his snub and would have put up her earphones if she'd remembered to bring them along. "Well, I'm sorry," he told her. "I just didn't think we ought to get all emotional about *shoes*. I do think the little kid in the tintype is probably the one in the graveyard. But so far we haven't got a bit of real evidence that he isn't right there, resting in peace. You see?"

After a minute Kat said sulkily, "I see. Then how about *you* have an idea for a change."

"I think I've got one. I'm back on the joke theory."

"Oh, Andy! You *can't* really believe . . . how would that explain the way he always disappeared? Just into thin air? If he was a real live boy just playing a dumb joke—"

"Listen, I bet these real live boys around here— not Jacob, the older ones who'd be really working the joke—I'll bet they know every foot of that hillside the way I know the back of my hand. *I* would, if I lived around here. I would've been exploring that rock and up in the woods there since I was born, almost. Playing I was an Indian, or—" Andy broke off, absorbed in the glories of growing up a country boy—glories unfairly denied boys born in central Portland.

"Maybe *you* would. But I've never seen a single

solitary Harper's Mill kid playing anywhere near those woods."

It was a minute before that penetrated Andy's daydream. When it did, he said in stupefaction, "You're right." The more he thought of it the more incredible it seemed. "How *come*? With all this good stuff right here under their noses—!" He swept a large gesture that took in the whole wild hill flanking the east side of the Buckles' lane, free for any boy's wandering, mostly "gov'munt property," Mrs. Sweet had told him once.

"Well, maybe they've got to do chores," Kat said. "At home, on their own farms. J.B. was busy as could be today. And Dawnelle picked bush beans all this morning—she was snapping 'em when we came. She has to help can them when her mom gets home from the Lodge."

"Oh. Yeah," said Andy, making some hasty re-adjustments in his idyllic vision of country life. "And come to think of it, Sweets' is the only farm close by. Some're three or four miles away." He looked again at the waiting, unexplored hillside, this time feeling rather sorry for it, with no boys busy making it their own. For that matter, he hadn't explored it himself—too many chores at the Lodge. "I guess farm kids have to stay home most of the time," he admitted. "Or—you know what? They might've heard tales of a ghost hanging around up here—that'd make them sort of avoid it. But they'd figure it was a perfect setup for a joke! I'm going to take a look around for a hiding place."

"Around the whole hillside?"

"No—just around the rock. I got wondering why he was always *there*, and no place else. Could be because there's a hiding place nearby."

Kat's enthusiasm was tepid. "Well, okay. But first let's stop in and tell Mr. Buckle about Aunt Henry's ghost, and the tintype."

When they reached the entrance to the Buckles' place, however, they saw a car, not Mr. Buckle's aged blue Chevy but an unfamiliar station wagon, drawn up outside the open door of the horse barn. As they watched, a short, squarish man came out leading one of the younger Belgians, followed by Mr. Buckle. Both were carefully observing the horse's gait, which showed a slight limp.

"Must be the vet," Andy said. "Never mind, we'll come back after we've checked out the rock." As they started on, he added, "You never know, we might find something there to report."

It seemed just one of those casual remarks.

CHAPTER THIRTEEN

"I don't understand what you think you'll find," Kat complained when they stood in the old spot in the lane, gazing up at the rock.

"The way Jacob vanished. Maybe."

"But you already went up there once, and looked all around."

"I didn't know what I was looking for then. I only thought—footprints or something. Today I'm going to look for a cave." Kat squinted at him in disbelief. He said impatiently, "Not a big, regular cave. I know there wouldn't be one of those." He shaded his eyes, peering up toward the rock. "Just some kind of hollow place or something, maybe right *under* the rock. I mean, if we can find just one little crack big enough for a nine-year-old kid to squirm into, so he'd *seem* to disappear, the joke theory is back in business."

Scrambling after him up the bank, Kat said rather crossly, "I don't think a little kid would keep squirming in and out of a hole just for somebody else's joke."

"Well, I don't think a real ghost would pick a place half a block from his grave to haunt."

The argument having reached a draw, if not agreement, they picked their way in silence through the brambles at the top of the bank and across the sparse knee-high grasses and weeds of the little glade. The ground was hard underfoot and fairly level. The whole place hummed with insects; sun and heat seemed to collect here as in a bowl. Above them, the rock loomed, casting an anvil-shaped shadow, transparent blue, that reached to the woods on its northeast side.

Andy stood for a moment eyeing it, sizing it up almost as a living adversary. It was the way he'd come to feel about it. Beaver Rock was a big, fat, buttoned-lip enigma twice the size of J.B.'s tractor and a hundred times as solid, and rooted to the whole mountain under these weeds—and it knew some kind of secret that he was going to find out if it took him the rest of his life. *That* was the way he felt about it.

So just watch out, here I come! he told it silently —and absurdly, but then nobody knew but him that he was standing here threatening a rock.

Kat, too, was standing quite still, for a different reason. "D'you suppose there's snakes?" she asked in a slightly quavery tone.

"Prob'ly. Garter snakes. They won't hurt you."

"But I don't like them *slithering*. They're so *sudden*!"

"Go stand in the shade, on the other side of the

rock," Andy told her impatiently. "They'd rather be in the sun. You would too, if your blood wasn't warm enough to keep you comfortable."

Kat's expression of uneasy dread abruptly changed to one of interest and deep compassion. "Is *that* why they always lie around on stone walls? Poor little things! Imagine always having cold feet!"

"They can't even imagine having feet," Andy said absently. He was prowling around the base of the rock, parting the grasses and salal, and occasionally kicking smaller rocks aside. As far as he could tell, that hulking great boulder was as solid in its socket as his molars in his jaw, and there wasn't a crevice underneath it anywhere. "Help me look!" he told Kat, who had gone around into the anvil of shade, her mind still on snakes.

"I really know they won't bite, or poison me or anything. Anyway not the ones around here. But Marsha Moore, at school, put her hand *right down* on one once, on a stone wall she was climbing up on, and . . . here's a sort of crack or something, Andy . . . and I've always thought, what if *I* did that, it would be so utterly *yucky*. Did you hear me?"

"Yeah, Marsha Moore put her hand down on a—"

"No, about the *crack*. It's more of a sort of little burrow or something, really. Maybe a fox lives there. Or a raccoon?" she hazarded as Andy arrived abruptly beside her.

It *was* a hole—or crevice—or burrow—or doll-sized cave—hard to tell which, or how far under the rock it went. All that showed was a patch of darker shadow, roughly triangular in shape, nearly hidden behind a clump of bracken. Andy fell to his knees and, reckless of whatever inhabitant might be waiting to defend its home and castle, thrust in his arm as far as it would go. His hand met no resistance. He stretched out flat and reached in farther, groped to right and left. Still no walls or roof—if it was a burrow it was for something a lot bigger than a fox. He pulled out his arm and rolled over to grin up at Kat triumphantly.

"It's a *cave*. I knew it! It's big enough for a kid the size of Jacob to hide there easy—I mean if he could get in," he added with a frowning second look at the arm-sized opening.

"That's a pretty big if," Kat muttered. She, too, was staring at the shadowed opening, looking half astonished, half in doubt. The doubt won out. "He couldn't, Andy," she said after a minute. "I don't think even a three-year-old could get through there. And this fern isn't even broken. If Jacob had been squirming in and out and in and out—"

"But that was a week or two ago. More! Last time we saw him, those writers were still at the Lodge—and they left July second. Today's the seventeenth! Plenty of time for a few bracken fronds to grow back. Only the hole *is* awful small."

Turning on his stomach again, Andy examined the opening at close range, and suddenly reached to the apex of the triangle to wiggle something.

"What is it?" demanded Kat, squatting down beside him and holding the fern aside.

"I dunno." Andy dropped his hand and peered at the left side of the crooked triangle, then at the right, which had been covered by the fern. "But doesn't this thing look kind of *built*?"

"What do you mean, 'built'?"

"Well, look." Leaning on his elbow, Andy traced with his finger some irregular cracks on the rough uneven face of the rock. "See? Like somebody's maybe stuffed smaller hunks of rock in here to kind of fill in the hole." His glance suddenly searched the weeds at the base of the rock, which shelved slightly inward in a low overhang. "Rocks like this!" he exclaimed, pouncing on a flattish chunk, obviously once part of Beaver Rock, lying loose under the shelf.

Further search turned up a great many fragments, some mere chips, some larger, many more webbed over by the network of tough grass runners and slowly turning into topsoil. If anybody had wanted to block that hole up, they'd have found ample material at hand. But it was a pretty expert job, and pretty subtly camouflaged, to be the impromptu work of a couple or three boys fixing up a practical joke. Andy reorganized himself into a more right-side-up position, and Kat pushed the bracken clear down and sat on it. Both of them stared at the dark opening, at the tracery of tiny cracks running over its edges, and then up at the massive side of Beaver Rock, whose "head" jutted out just over them, a black cutout against the summer sky. The whole rock was weathering, eternal as it first had seemed; there were cracks and shingly-looking places all over it—great solid lumps interspersed with layers that were little more than crumbs held together by habit and the weight above.

Andy was suddenly on his feet. "I'm going up to the Lodge for my grubbing hoe," he said.

"Andy! What?" Kat scrambled up too.

"Just sit there and wait. I'll be right back."

He was already stumbling across the glade, plunging down the bank to the path. I probably can't make a dent in it, he was warning himself. But he meant to find out more about the hole before he was half an hour older.

He was back inside of fifteen minutes, breathless but no less determined to enlarge the opening until it was big enough to take Kat's head and shoulders, if not his. He had brilliantly thought to detour by the cottage and grab the flashlight, which he tossed to Kat with a flourish.

"Oh, neat! I'd never have remembered that," Kat exclaimed in tones of quite satisfactory respect. "Nobody's gone in or out," she reported. "I mean like foxes or snakes. But listen, what if some animal does live there? With little babies? We'll be destroying their home."

That's their lookout, Andy thought with a feeling of ruthlessness that surprised even him. He said only, "I won't destroy it. But I'm going to see inside." He raised the grubbing hoe into its salal-slaughtering position, hesitated, then reluctantly lowered it for more cautious tactics. If there really was a cave in there, he didn't want to fill it with rubble before he even got a glimpse. Turning the hoe to its picklike end, he tapped lightly but insistently at a nick where a spiderweb of little cracks came together. He was rewarded by seeing a chip fly out, and the nick enlarge to a pit the size of his tool's point. He tap-tapped again, with good results, then fitted the pick of the grubbing hoe into the gap he had made, and pried.

The whole left side of the triangle tumbled to the ground, the largest rock bouncing malevolently onto his toe.

"*Ow*," he exploded, hopping around on the other foot and flinging the grubbing hoe aside. For the moment it took the pain to subside to ignorable dimensions, he could do nothing but gnash his teeth and squeeze his eyes shut against it. When he opened them, Kat was down on her stomach, peering into the much-enlarged hole.

He gasped, "D'you see anything?"

"Not really." Kat wriggled a little farther forward and abruptly retreated, flapping a hand in front of her face and uttering "Phuhs" and "Phloos" of revulsion. "Spiderwebs! Plaaa! Plah! Gimme something to clear them away."

Andy tore a frond off the bracken and put it in her back-stretched hand, then limped over to where she had left the flashlight. By the time she had done a thorough job of clearing the entrance of every possible lingering web, he was bursting with impatience. He snatched the frond out of her hand.

"That's good enough! Here, take the flash and *look*."

Kat obeyed. After a moment she elbowed her way forward until most of her head was inside, along with the hand holding the light.

"Well?" demanded Andy.

"We need new batteries in this thing," Kat reported, her voice echoing hollowly.

"You mean you can't see *anything*? Let me try."

"No, no, I can see a little. Got to let my eyes get used to it. . . . Looks like there's just a kind of— space, with dirt and rock chips and stuff like that on the floor, and the underside of the big rock above. Goes quite a way back, but it's too low for even a beetle to stand up straight back there."

Andy was suffering an intolerable letdown. "What about the front part? Isn't that big enough for a kind of skinny kid to hide in?"

"Well, maybe, over here on this side. . . ." Kat squirmed through a series of adjustments that involved changing the flashlight to the other hand and lying on the other shoulder. "Yeah, it's a little higher over here. Only there's something—"

There was dead silence for a moment, long enough for Andy to prompt her. "Something *what?*"

"Something—there," came the hollow, hesitant reply.

"Well what *is* it? You mean an animal or something?" Andy felt he couldn't stand this. "Listen, let *me* look."

"It's just—I can't tell. Not an animal. Wait a minute, maybe I can . . . " More squirming, and this time by some masterpiece of contortion, Kat got her other arm in, and Andy could tell she was straining to reach something far to her right, only to give up with a defeated sigh. "No use. Hand me a stick or something, maybe I can—"

Andy was already scrabbling for the discarded bracken frond, stripping everything off the stem, which was stiff toward the lower end and as thick as his little finger. He threaded it between Kat's shoulder and the rocky edge of the entrance, saying, "Will this do?"

"Yeah, if I can get hold—okay, got it. Now all I have to do is . . . "

More straining and reaching, a little grunt of satisfaction, then—silence. Andy, eagerly watching the visible parts of his twin in the absence of anything more informative, saw her body go as still as a movie suddenly halted on one frame. Then, abruptly, the movie was switched to double speed reverse; Kat emerged backwards from her hole like a lizard flicking from its crack, stumbled to her feet and rocketed into Andy, clinging to him with a gasping sob.

"Kat! *Kat*! What's the matter, what is it?" Frantic, Andy gave her a shake, then dived toward the hole himself and struggled in vain to get far enough in to see something.

"Andy, wait! Don't! Don't look!"

She was beside him, tugging at his shoulders, her teeth chattering and her breath coming in great uneven gulps. He sat up abruptly and put his arms around her.

"Shut up, it can't be that bad," he muttered, patting. "Come on. Cool it. Cool it. Just *tell* me. What was it, a dead rat or something?"

"No, no, no—an old—sort of sack, or rags or something—sort of rolled up, so I couldn't tell . . .

so I was trying to pull back the edge so I could see, and—and I finally reached it with the stick, and—" Kat swallowed convulsively.

"So come on—*and*—what was in it, then?"

Kat's eyes met his and were suddenly drowned in tears. "Bones," she whispered. Her voice went high and out of control. "A little skull. A whole . . . little skel—skel—" Abruptly she covered her face with her hands and sobbed despairingly.

Andy sat rigid, his hand still absently patting her, feeling as if all his flesh were undergoing some sort of transformation into another substance; it crawled and shrank and went numb and then clammy with patches of cold sweat. He opened his mouth wide and took a gulp of air through it and after a sort of gasp that made his chest jump, managed to get back on his usual breathing schedule.

"Kat," he said, in an approximation of his ordinary voice. There was a sort of muffled squeak he took to be response. "I'm going to go look. I may have to knock out a few more rocks."

She immediately made feeble standing-up motions, keeping one arm crooked over her eyes and groping toward her jeans pocket. He helped her up, led her free of possible flying rock chips, and said, "now just stay there."

"I *never* have a Kleenex when I want one!" she quavered crossly.

"Maybe you can use a leaf," Andy said. He was

already retrieving his grubbing hoe and advancing to the opening, looking for another possible point of leverage. A few experimental taps on the untouched edge—the edge nearest Kat's fearful discovery—revealed a loosened stone the size of his fist, which supported one the size of his head. With due caution he freed both, knocked away the chips from the base, and tossing aside his hoe, got down again on his stomach.

The opening now accepted his head and shoulders as easily as it had Kat's before. The flashlight was still lying where she had dropped it, still throwing a beam of feeble, brownish light across the chip-strewn dirt floor of the cave, which was more like a wedge-shaped slit under the big rock. Taking a firm grip on himself, he shone the light directly to his right, into the large end of the wedge.

There was the roll of rags, or sack, or . . . he could see why she hadn't known what to call it. The edge she had managed to flip back with the stick was lying in shreds. Probably, Andy thought, the whole roll would disintegrate at a touch.

And there too, of course, only half revealed by the turned-back edge but plain enough, were the little bones and the skull.

Andy looked for a long moment, and found he had looked enough, forever. He started backing out, the flashlight darting beams every which way in his moving hand. He paused to turn it off and found himself peering at some little object caught in its beam. It lay just his side of the shredded sacking—no doubt tossed there when Kat flipped the edge back.

He reached for it, switched off the light and backed out of the hole.

He got to his feet. As Kat came over to him, he opened his hand and they both stared at the tiny object on his palm.

"It looks like . . . what is it?" Kat whispered.

"I dunno for sure. Never saw one before."

But they both knew, really. It was a shoe button. They had found Jacob.

CHAPTER FOURTEEN

M r. Buckle had to be told immediately, of course—vet or no vet. And once Andy had decreed that they must not both go, leaving the little cave open and unprotected, it became obvious who was going to stay there all alone and guard it.

Kat went for Mr. Buckle.

Andy, sitting on a low hump of rock protruding among the weeds near the entrance, simply waited, his elbows propped on his knees, his mind in neutral, everything in him taking time out, especially his emotions, which felt as if they had had enough strenuous exercise for the next three years.

Once he moved an arm—heavily, because it seemed to weigh a lot more than usual—and fumbled in his pocket for the shoe button. Again he stared at it on his palm, trying to *realize*, trying to cope with what it was—Jacob's own personal shoe button, maybe the same exact one that had pulled the shoe tight over the ankle, in the old picture. There it was, a little black half sphere with a loop of sturdy wire sticking out of the flat side—probably shiny once, now dulled with time—and

Jacob's own living fingers had probably worked it into its buttonhole a hundred times. Andy tried to grasp that, to make it real; but his grasping powers still seemed to be out to lunch. He ended up restoring the button to his pocket, feeling intensely protective and private about it, as if it were somebody's innermost secret that had been entrusted to him, but apologetic because he couldn't really comprehend.

And once a new thought occurred to him and he straightened on his rocky seat, looked hopefully around the empty glade, and said in a low voice, "Jacob?" He saw nothing, nobody; but he went ahead, almost in a whisper. "Jacob, I'm doing what I said. I'm working on it. I'll get it done."

It made him feel like a fool, but somehow a little steadier. He went back to merely sitting, letting himself merge with the humming, sun-drenched, grass-smelling afternoon.

And then Kat was back, with Mr. Buckle and the vet, too, scrambling up the bank after her. Andy stood up, encountered a look from Mr. Buckle that was a whole anxious question—not about the cave but about himself. He answered it with a nod, muttering, "I'm okay." Kat was not, yet, though he could see it had helped her to run for reinforcements, to do something.

Mr. Buckle rumbled, "Pretty rough experience for you two." He jerked a thumb at his companion, the same short, square man they had seen in the barnyard. "Doc Greves. He was right there handy, seeing to Big Boy—brought 'im along as witness. This here's your cave, I reckon."

He got down on all fours, the vet squatting beside him. Andy gave him the flashlight, said "It's way over to the right, near the front," then went to stand beside Kat, letting his arm touch hers. She leaned against it, still quivering a little, and breathing hard from her run, but gradually steadier as they waited.

"By golly," Mr. Buckle said under his breath. He drew back, handed the flashlight to the vet, who leaned into the cave in his turn. After a moment they both stood up, exchanged a long look.

"Well, I'm ready to swear to it in a court of law," said Dr. Greves. His voice was unexpectedly high, and melodious, as if he might break into song like an Irish tenor at any moment. "That's a human skeleton, it's a child's, and it's been there a time. A good long time. I wouldn't wanta say how long."

Andy stepped over to them and produced the shoe button. "We found this in there—did Kat tell you?"

"Yes, but I want to see it." Mr. Buckle took the button and slowly shook his head. "Takes me back. My grandpa still wore button shoes when I was a youngster. Had a buttonhook with a silver handle

—I remember it plain as day." He handed the button to Dr. Greves. "There's probably more of these in there. Help date it pretty close."

The vet studied it, returned it to Andy. "Look to you like the ones in that tintype?"

So Kat had told them about that, too. Well, that made it simpler. "As near as I could see," he said. To Mr. Buckle he added, "What do we do now?"

"Get another outside witness, first of all—I should've brought Ellerton along in the beginning, but he was way yonder in the poultry house, and I didn't wanna . . . we'll fetch him now, though. You and Kat can run down there while I phone the sheriff. Doc'll stay here so's he can swear nobody's been messing with so much as a grass blade since that hidey-hole was discovered. Come on."

So back they went down the lane, the three of them. "If we're gonna keep trottin' back and forth, I better hitch up," Mr. Buckle said to Kat with a smile and a penetrating glance.

Checking up on her, thought Andy, who had being doing so himself. But she was okay—her answering smile a little shaky, but her freckles not showing so plainly or her eyes so oversized.

He said, "What'll the sheriff do?"

"Probably send over a local deppity till he can get an officer up here from Oregon City. . . . Somebody'll have to be on the spot all the time till they're ready to . . . move the little fella."

"Where will they move him?" Kat asked quickly. "You mean back to—back to—"

"No, no, not back to where he belongs, not yet, honey. They got no authority to do that. Anyhow they'll have to get their official squint at that cave, and take their pictures or whatever they're gonna do, and the sheriff's man's gonna want to ask you two a coupla questions. I think you ought to stay in the house with Mrs. Buckle till your mom can get down here from the Lodge to be with you."

"But she's not at the Lodge," the twins said together.

Andy realized from the dismayed sound of Kat's voice that she, too, had just remembered it. He said, "Has Dodie got to be here? She's clear down in Portland—won't be back till late tomorrow."

"No-o-o . . . But I think you oughta call her right away. Kinda put her in the picture," said Mr. Buckle. "She might want to come back earlier."

"Oh, *yes*," Kat agreed fervently. "We will! I *want* to."

Mr. Buckle was thoughtful as they turned into his barnyard and started for the house. "Tell you what, though," he said after a moment. "Let's hold off just a few minutes. We'll locate Ellerton, and I'll let Mrs. Buckle know what's going on. Then I'll drive you up to the Lodge to phone your mom. I'll call the sheriff from there, too. We got a party line." He met Andy's glance of incomprehension with a wryly cocked eyebrow.

"Means there's nine other families share our line. And when one of us picks up a receiver all the rest can hear a kinda little 'ping' sound in their phone boxes. And right about then, a lot of 'em pick up *their* receivers—human nature bein' what it is. Just don't wanta miss anything."

Kat was staring at him. "You mean they can all hear whatever you're saying? To whoever you called?"

"Every word, honey." Mr. Buckle smiled reassuringly. "So we'll just use the phone at the Lodge. Don't want the whole county knowing our business before we're braced for it."

Would they ever be braced for it, Andy wondered, as his imagination suddenly—and apprehensively—got busy on what the next few days might be like. He found he wanted as badly as Kat to phone Dodie, get her back here. Moreover he wanted the tough Campion Hall Dodie—the one who could silence Mrs. Corey-who-cooks with one unvarnished *yes*. Not that he was exactly looking forward to what Mr. Buckle called "putting her in the picture." He and Kat would have to tell her the whole Jacob story now—and try to explain why they hadn't mentioned it before. But never mind. He'd do it.

As it happened, Ellerton was just coming out of the house when they reached it. Mr. Buckle took him aside and muttered—for quite a while. That was okay. Andy found he didn't mind Ellerton knowing any part of it—all of it—and besides, as caretaker of that graveyard it was his business to know.

The moment Ellerton's serious, greenish gaze could leave Mr. Buckle's lips it went to Kat, and Andy, like a kind of promise. All he said, in his muted voice, was, "Don't you worry. I'll look after things up at the rock." But he meant, Andy knew, that he wouldn't let anything happen they wouldn't like—or weren't informed about.

Not that we could stop it, Andy thought helplessly as he watched Ellerton's slight figure cross the barnyard toward the lane. He didn't even know what "it" might be, or exactly what to expect, but only that he was resisting the immediate future with everything in him, and the more he didn't know about it, the more his stomach tried to tie in knots.

He and Kat waited around outside while Mr. Buckle went into the kitchen, where Mrs. Buckle was creating something that smelled wonderfully like roasting pork and reminded Andy sharply that it must be getting on toward four o'clock. In a very short time he came out again, followed as far as the door by Mrs. Buckle, who was saying, "Mercy, yes! Whole town'll be onto it soon enough. . . . You poor kids. What a thing to happen. Now listen —come on back and stay here till your mother gets home, you hear? We got plenty of supper, extra beds if need be. Don't stay up yonder all by yourselves."

"All right," Kat agreed immediately, but Andy said, "Once we get hold of Dodie, she could probably make it back by dinnertime. Thanks a lot, though."

Mrs. Buckle nodded and turned back into the house; Mr. Buckle, leading the way to the shed where his old blue Chevy waited, murmured, "All I told her was just—what you found up there. Get around to the rest of the story later, when I've got more time."

Andy darted a glance at him as they climbed into the car. "I was sort of wondering—how she'd feel about—well, ghosts and things."

"I'm not real sure myself. She's a mighty down-to-earth, practical sort of woman. But she'll keep her opinions in the family. That I do know." As he turned toward the county road Mr. Buckle added, "She asked me how you ever happened to stumble on that cave—all these years, nobody ever saw it before. How did you?"

"We went looking for it. At least for some place a little kid might hide, after pretending to be Jacob." Andy explained about his joke theory. "I was only trying to do what you said—find evidence *against*."

"Instead it was evidence *for*," Kat said.

Mr. Buckle smiled rather grimly as the car jounced over the last of the gravel onto pavement. "And a lot more of it than any of us bargained for. Don't know whether I'm glad or sorry."

Kat said fiercely, "I'm glad. If it'll get him back his bed."

"*If*," muttered Andy, trying unsuccessfully to envision the days ahead.

Mr. Buckle said nothing.

The Lodge office was just off the big lounge, where Mrs. Sweet was shampooing the rug in front of the fireplace, being talked to by Mrs. Corey leaning in the dining-room doorway gesturing with a giant spoon. So Andy set the switchboard to assure an outside line for the cottage, and they went over there.

"Help yourself," Kat offered, waving to the kitchen phone. Andy subsided onto a stool, waiting tensely while Mr. Buckle looked up the sheriff's number in the curly-paged telephone book that hung beside the phone. He couldn't imagine how even Mr. Buckle was ever going to explain it all to a perfect stranger.

It was simple. He made no effort to explain. "This is Harry C. Buckle, on Buckles' Lane just off the county road about half a mile north of Harper's

Mill. Coupla kids found a skeleton on my property about half an hour ago. . . . That's right, just bones. . . . Oh, yes, they're human. A child. Vet happened to be here—he vouches for that. . . . No, I don't think you'll find there's any connection. With that that or any other modern crime. . . . Well, because I've got a notion they've been there a good long while. . . . Yeah, I figured you'd want to. Who's your deppity around here nowadays? . . . Well, Elmer'll know how to get to my place. . . . Yes, vet's up there now, and my brother-in-law. . . . Yep. All right." After this masterful performance he replaced the receiver and said calmly, "Your turn."

But then they couldn't get hold of Dodie.

"She's not *there*?" Kat repeated blankly when Andy hung up after the eighth or ninth ring. "But she must be! The roofing man's working. Where would she go?"

"Anywhere! Grocery store, hairdresser, downtown, Campion Hall—"

Kat grabbed a possibility as it passed. "Campion Hall. She said she wanted to get some stuff from her office."

Andy tried Campion Hall. He tried Dodie's closest friend. He even tried her cousin Florrie, with whom she never willingly spent fifteen minutes if she could avoid it. No answer anywhere. He tried home again, in case he'd dialed a wrong number at first—and then again, visualizing with surreal clarity the sand-colored phone standing between his and Kat's sixth-grade pictures on the living room desk, the white wall phone in the kitchen beside the cluttered bulletin board, both ringing their heads off in an empty house. If the roof man was still working, he'd be wondering who was so persistent, but he wouldn't think it had anything to do with him.

"But she must be *somewhere*," Kat wailed as he hung up with a final exasperated sigh.

"We'll just have to wait till this evening and try again."

Mr. Buckle, who had been standing silently by the door, said, "I'll bring you back up here anytime you say."

"But—she might walk in the house any minute!" Kat protested. "Do we have to leave? . . . Oh, that's right—the deputy, and all that."

"Deppity needn't concern you. I'll take him up to the rock when he comes, and Ellerton and Doc Greves can go off duty." Mr. Buckle glanced at his watch. "Gonna take the sheriff's officer an hour or so, even if he left the minute I called. Stay here and keep trying—say, till five o'clock. I'll pick you up then."

"No need, we'll walk down." Andy glanced at Kat. "You aren't scared, are you?"

"Of *Jacob*? No!"

"I meant of—walking past the . . . place."

But Kat shook her head, her lips tight together, her eyes down. So Mr. Buckle told them to plan on supper at his house, and went away.

After a silent few minutes, during which they sat in a state of suspended animation, unable to imagine anything else worth doing, Andy reached again for the phone. Again it rang, and rang, and rang.

CHAPTER FIFTEEN

At five minutes of five Andy locked the cottage door and he and Kat headed down through the woods. "Never mind, we'll get hold of her sooner or later," Andy said. "She's bound to go back to the house to sleep."

"But are *we* going back to the cottage?" Kat asked rather tremulously as they alternately plunged and picked their way down the familiar steep path. "Mrs. Buckle thought we ought to sleep at their house."

"Do you want to?"

"I don't know," Kat said. "I want Dodie to come. I wish it was all over."

Andy did, too—he wished he even had some idea of what was going to happen. He'd never set eyes on a sheriff's officer in his life and didn't want to now.

When he saw this one, though, standing with Mr. Buckle on the path below the rock, his anxiety retreated to a more comfortable distance. Officer Cameron was a solid young man with dark, direct eyes and several unmanageable cowlicks that gave him a reassuringly normal look. Mr. Buckle introduced the twins, adding, after a penetrating glance at their expressions, "No luck on the phone, I see. We'll try after supper. Mrs. Buckle's put your names in the pot." He nodded toward his companion. "Officer Cameron needs a little information now. Just the facts," he added casually.

The officer cleared his throat apologetically, and said, more or less to Kat, "We'll go down to the house right away. I just need you to confirm that this is the site. Where you found the evidence."

The evidence. He meant Jacob, Andy supposed. He and Kat both nodded. There were several strangers doing things up around the rock; he couldn't help darting nervous glances at them.

"It's the other folks from the sheriff's office," Mr. Buckle told him. "Photographer, couple of detectives, medical examiner. And—I'm not too happy to say—a reporter from *The Oregonian*. Happened to be hanging around the sheriff's office with nothing better to do just when my call came in."

Officer Cameron obviously caught the note of vexation in his voice. "We can't prevent the media people following along, if they hear about it. Or doing their job."

"Oh, I know it, I know it," Mr. Buckle grumbled. "Just a complication we don't need. I'll talk to him. But don't *you*," he commanded Andy and Kat. "Not till your mom's here. Why don't I just get it over right now, then maybe he'll leave. You all go on."

He clambered up the bank, which was already beginning to look as if it had stairsteps in it from all the traffic, and the officer turned to start down the lane. The twins hung back, watching the men around the rock.

"What are they going to do?" Kat whispered.

"I dunno," Andy muttered.

Officer Cameron said, "Something the matter?"

Andy faced him. "D'you know what's going to happen to—" He bit his tongue to keep from saying "Jacob." "To uh—"

"To the evidence? That'll be turned over to the medical examiner. He'll have custody from this point on."

"On till when?" persisted Andy. He wished Officer Cameron wouldn't keep saying "the evidence." It made Jacob seem so much less . . . like himself.

The officer shrugged. "Till the case is closed."

And when would that be? Andy didn't like the idea of Jacob's little bones being taken clear away somewhere—for nobody knew how long. He wasn't sure he could stand it.

Kat ventured, "Where will—where will the medical officer—keep . . ."

"In the evidence property room. Sheriff's office."

A picture formed instantly in Andy's mind of a

small, ill-lit storeroom with a dirty window and probably cobwebs, full of shelves and tables cluttered with evidence—every kind of thing from rusty revolvers to old letters and disintegrating clothes showing bullet holes. And *this* was where they were going to put Jacob.

But there wasn't anything to do about it. About anything. He exchanged a bleak glance with Kat and resolutely started down the lane after Officer Cameron, trying to brace himself for the coming interview. Just the facts. He'd got Mr. Buckle's message, loud and clear. He hoped Kat had.

There was nobody around the house or barns, though they could hear Mrs. Buckle clattering pans back in the kitchen. Officer Cameron gestured rather awkwardly toward the front porch, cool and shaded this time of day. "We could just sit there on the steps. All right with you?"

Andy nodded. He had a notion Officer Cameron wasn't much good with kids—he seemed less at his ease than they did. The thought was relaxing. He and Kat sat down close together on the second step and waited for him to begin.

"So. Just tell me in your own words how you— found the evidence," he said, perching stiffly on the third step, and producing a battered-looking little notebook and a pencil.

Kat spoke up instantly. "We were playing near the rock. I noticed a kind of crack. We thought some little animal might live there. But Andy said somebody'd walled it up, and he—knocked the wall down."

Andy stole a glance at her, marveling. Just the facts. She must have been rehearsing all the way down the lane.

"That's about it," he confirmed, deadpan.

"No idea, I suppose, of how the evidence got there. I mean—what happened."

Andy opened his mouth to say no, found he couldn't, and closed it again, darting a look at Kat, who was chewing her lower lip and staring earnestly toward the lane.

Officer Cameron said in surprise, "You do have some idea?" In the silence his eyes moved from one to the other of them, alert and intelligent. He had suddenly lost his awkward air. "Maybe you better tell me."

Now what? thought Andy—but already the cat was half out of the bag, just from not answering quickly enough. Anyway how was anything ever going to turn out right for Jacob if somebody didn't speak up about that grave?

"Look," said Officer Cameron. "I'm not going to arrest you or anything. Medical examiner said the evidence looked pretty old—probably nothing to do with any recent crime. But if you know different—"

"Oh, no, I don't know different," Andy said quickly.

"Or have heard anybody talking—"

"Oh, no," Kat told him.

He was silent a moment, trying to read their faces. "Let me put it this way. If you can shed any light on this investigation, it's your duty to say so. You *do* know something?"

Kat looked a little scared by the mention of "duty," but went on studying her fingernails. Andy said stolidly, "We think we do. But we don't think anybody's going to believe us. So we'd rather not say anything—just now."

"When can I expect a statement?" asked Officer Cameron with equal stolidity.

He was a very persistent man—and obviously he intended to keep asking questions until he got some sort of answer. His voice had taken on an impersonal, official quality that Andy found dismaying and Kat, apparently, terrifying. She jerked to her feet and backed off, saying, "Do we *have* to say something?"

Andy sprang up at once to range himself beside her, and Officer Cameron slowly stood up too, looking embarrassed. "Take it easy. Sit down. I didn't mean . . . I'm only trying to find out about this. It's my job."

Andy tried to relax. "Would it be okay," he

asked, "if we wait just till Mr. Buckle shows up? I'd sort of like to . . . see what he thinks."

Officer Cameron hesitated, then said, "Yes, that would be okay."

They resumed their seats on the steps. There was an uncomfortable, waiting silence, during which it became clear why Officer Cameron's notebook looked so exhausted. His square, strong hands kept rolling it into a tight little tube, loosening it a bit, then tightening it up, obviously without engaging his mind, which seemed to be busy elsewhere.

A car came bouncing down the lane, stopped with a scrunch of gravel at the driveway to disgorge Mr. Buckle, then took off toward the county road in a cloud of dust. Everybody stood up again. Officer Cameron stuffed the notebook in his pocket, stepped forward to meet Mr. Buckle and said without preliminaries, "The kids here know something they don't want to tell. Seems you know it too."

Mr. Buckle stopped, looked at all three faces, then said slowly, "I know what they know. Yes. Because they told me."

"You didn't mention it before."

"No. It's their story. I thought what they said should be up to them. . . . Sorry I took so long, kids. That *Oregonian* fella kept me."

Andy said in distress, "We *did* just tell the facts. But then he asked us—straight out—"

Officer Cameron broke in, stepping in front of Mr. Buckle. "You understand that to conceal—"

"Son, we're not trying to shield any criminals," Mr. Buckle said soothingly. "But it's all so kind of peculiar—it's a hard story to tell." To the twins he said, "Think we better try?"

"I think we've got to," Andy said. "Because if we don't—"

Kat nodded, and Mr. Buckle said, "Well, I'm with you. Go ahead."

Andy assumed he was nominated, took a long breath, and started on the tale—about the boy on the hillside, the one in the tintype, the one in the grave, their conclusions about the "bed," and their reasons for prowling around Beaver Rock.

Officer Cameron's expression grew more and more stunned as he listened, his dark, puzzled gaze half alarmed, as it moved from Andy to Kat to Mr. Buckle and, when the story was finished, back to Andy.

"I'm supposed to believe that?" he asked at last.

"Well, I said you wouldn't," Andy said hopelessly.

"But—do *you*?"

"I've got to. It happened."

Kat said, "It did. Honest."

Officer Cameron swung around to Mr. Buckle,

who shrugged. "These are truthful kids. What's more I've seen a little boy mighty like that myself —off and on for years. Always up by the rock. There's the matter of the shoe button, too. I gather you found more of those."

Officer Cameron said reluctantly, "Eleven altogether."

Andy's hand slid of itself into his pocket; his fingers closed around the twelfth. He intended to refuse categorically to give it up, to allow it to be carried off with the others to that unfriendly-sounding evidence property room, where probably nobody would ever think of it again. Officer Cameron had noticed the movement; his dark, troubled gaze clung to Andy's face a moment, but he didn't issue any commands. Instead, he heaved a sigh and turned to Mr. Buckle.

"I don't know how to figure this one, and that's a fact," he said abruptly. "None of the rules fit."

"I believe you," Mr. Buckle assured him. "You want to call time out for a talk with the sheriff?"

Officer Cameron frowned, his firm, shaven cheeks going a little red. "No, I'm in charge. It's just—I've got to find some way to—make it regular. You won't mind signing written statements?"

"We'll cooperate in any way you want," Mr. Buckle told him. "Within reason," he amended after a glance at Andy's jaw. "You understand, the three of us had some plans of our own about that grave, and this thing today seems to me good reason to go ahead with 'em. What would the official attitude be about that?''

Andy waited anxiously for the answer, but Officer Cameron seemed not to know what to say.

"The bed was *stolen*," Andy reminded him.

Kat said, "Jacob told us himself. He said, 'They just *stole* it. It was mine.' ''

"Yes, well, I don't think there'd be an official attitude." Officer Cameron sounded harried. "I mean it'd be up to me. It's my case." He spoke as if he wished it were somebody else's—anybody else's.

"Then how do *you* feel about it?" Kat ventured.

Officer Cameron communed with himself, staring glumly at the barn. Then he said, "Seems to me it's your own business, what you do about a grave in that pioneer cemetery. Yours and this local group that I understand administers it. Far as I *know*, or *can prove*, there's no connection with the evidence found today near Beaver Rock. None at all." His shoulders relaxed a little. He turned to Mr. Buckle with relief. "So it's over to you."

Mr. Buckle blinked. "Not doubting your word, officer, but there must be some legal fuss or other about opening a grave."

"Oh. I can tell you the procedure for *that*." Officer Cameron was on firm ground now. "You

need permission from next-of-kin or the most
directly descended relatives. Or else from the caretaker of the cemetery."

There was an astonished silence.

"That's *all?*" Andy was gaping at him.

"I thought there'd be a sight more to it myself,"
Mr. Buckle commented. "Well, we can locate descendants—don't know how direct . . ."

Kat was whispering excitedly to Andy, "The
caretaker—that's Ellerton!"

"Yeah—but that Historical Society runs it.
Ellerton just keeps the weeds down and the stray
dogs chased off, remember?"

"Oh, yeah. Too bad," Kat muttered. "I bet he'd
be on our side."

"Maybe the Sweets will, too—they must be the
'descendants.' "

Aunt Henry, Andy was thinking. *She* would, for
sure. And Mrs. Sweet—no, it'd only be Mr. Sweet.
And J.B. and Dawnelle. Would they mind? Surely
they wouldn't mind. Not if we told them about the
shoe button. Not if we explained.

By seven that evening, when Officer Cameron
at last departed, leaving the deputy to guard the
"site" but taking along the two detectives, the
medical examiner, and—presumably—"the evidence," Andy felt as though the day had been going

on for several weeks. It was actually hard to remember back to that morning, when Dodie was just driving away, and he and Kat had yet to set foot inside the graveyard fence. It was harder to believe there ever had been such a relatively carefree time.

Mrs. Buckle, fully informed by now, was keeping her own troubled counsel. She devoted herself to serving the meal and rather mechanically urging everybody to eat—though nobody paid much attention. Kat's appetite had departed along with the sheriff's car. Andy needed no urging; he had suddenly found himself so ravenous he could have eaten the glazed forget-me-nots off his plate. Ellerton ate little and said less. None of them talked more than necessary to agree on the program for the evening: first, back to the cottage to phone Dodie once more; then to the Christmas tree farm to confer with the family of Martin Sweet.

"And I won't go, Harry," Mrs. Buckle said firmly. "Me'n Ellerton'll stay here and wash up the dishes and keep out of it. Going to be too many people discussing this from now on as it is."

"Afraid Ellerton can't keep *clear* out of it," Mr. Buckle said. "He's caretaker up yonder—member of that Historical Society, too."

Andy felt a leap of hope; his gaze riveted on Ellerton's face. Kat's had, too. But Ellerton only said in his usual soft, unemphatic voice, "I wouldn't wanta butt in, Harry. Family ought to have the say." He got up and took his plate to the sink.

So it was up to the Sweets.

It'll be all right, Andy told himself again. And later, when they'd spent another frustrating half hour at the cottage trying in vain to reach Dodie, he told Kat, too, in his sternest tones, that *everything would be all right*. "We'll find out tomorrow where she's been all this time, and it'll be real logical, and we'll wonder why we didn't think of it. Nothing's *happened* to her, how could it, just since this morning?"

"She could've got run over or something," Kat retorted tearfully.

"Listen, Dodie has more sense than to walk in front of a moving car. Now put a lid on it. Mr. Buckle's waiting to go to the Sweets'. And *that'll* be all right, too."

CHAPTER SIXTEEN

And it *was* all right—about the Sweets. Aunt Henry was instantly on their side, of course. Dawnelle joined her right away. Mrs. Sweet and J.B., after a good deal of boggling at the idea of a ghost, were won over by the tintype and the shoe button.

Martin Sweet alone held back. He was a big, dark-haired man who didn't say much or smile often, and at first Andy found him gruff and rather daunting; he could tell from Kat's expression that she did, too. But the longer he watched, the more convinced he became that, like Dawnelle, Mr. Sweet was just bashful around strangers, taken aback by what he was hearing, and slow to make up his mind. He listened closely to what everybody was saying, occasionally shifted uneasily in his chair or moved his oversized feet, and looked thoroughly distressed. It was plain he was swayed by the persuasiveness of the shoe button, and uncomfortable in the role of solitary holdout. But he was even more so with the outlandish idea of opening a grave.

Aunt Henry finally lost patience. "Laws, Martin,

'twon't do any harm just to spade out some dirt and look! We can put it right back if we need to!"

"Well, I know that, Auntie, but doggone it—"

"Daddy, *please*," implored Dawnelle.

This apparently was the one argument he could not resist; after a long, helpless look at her, he gave in. "Okay, okay, I'll go along. But it won't be us that decides it," he added. "We're not direct descendants. There aren't any. Not a one. That boy died before he got a chance to raise a family."

"Yes, but . . ." Andy looked at Aunt Henry, who was inconveniently taking one of her little naps. "I thought she said Jacob's father was her grandfather's brother."

"Step-brother," Mr. Sweet told him. "Come right down to it, we're no real kin at all."

Mr. Buckle pursed his lips in a silent whistle. "That sorta changes things, doesn't it?" he said thoughtfully.

Step-brother, thought Andy. He remembered now, Jacob himself had said I *don't have any brother*. "But does that matter?" he demanded. "A step-brother's part of the family. If Sweets are the only relations he's got—"

"You're forgettin' the Harper's Mill Historical Society," Mr. Buckle put in. "I've got a notion this is about where they step in. I was hoping we could get around that."

"Why?" asked Andy.

"Because Len Harper's the president."

There was a startled silence. "Leonard Harper the *egg man?*" Kat almost wailed, and Andy felt his stomach hit bottom.

The whole conference fell apart right then.

"That man!" said Mrs. Sweet with a disapproving sniff. "We'll never get him to agree to anything!"

"Not if he knows I'm in favor of it," muttered Mr. Buckle grimly.

Aunt Henry, who had awakened refreshed, uttered one of her little cackles. "He'll say it's heathenish," she predicted with relish. "Laws, how he'll take on!"

Everybody began to comment. Andy realized that the general mood in the room, like his own, was that of having run into a concrete wall. Len Harper, they all seemed certain, would welcome the chance to block any project approved by Harry Buckle or Harry's friends.

"But it's us he has the grudge against," Andy protested.

J.B. said, "You and half the town. But the line forms behind Mr. Buckle. Anything he favors, Len Harper's down on."

"Then how about—you sort of pretend you *don't* really favor it?" Kat suggested.

That brought another cackle from Aunt Henry, and a smile from even Mr. Buckle. But he shook his head. "I've never been a good liar. 'Bout the best I can do is keep a real low profile, and pretend I haven't got much opinion one way or the other."

"Anyway," Mr. Sweet said heavily, "I suspect it's up to a Sweet to do the talkin'. I'll go see Len first thing in the morning—on my way to work. Get it over with. Won't do much good."

"But you'll *try*, Daddy?"

"Dawnie, I'll put it to him fair and square. But you know Len."

It was a glum ride back to the Buckles'.

Kat broke the silence at last by saying tragically, "This is all because I didn't want to buy his eggs!"

"No, no, Kat honey—it's just the nature of the beast. Why, he still talks about that fool parade." Mr. Buckle sighed as he turned from the county road into his lane. "I never thought it'd ever matter one way or the other what Len Harper thought of me. You can't smooth things over with a fella like that. He won't let you. He likes his grudges. I always just figured it was hurting him more'n me. But I don't like it hurting you two. Makes me feel pretty bad."

"Doesn't matter about us—it's Jacob," Andy said numbly. The failure had been so abrupt, and seemed so final, that he was still trying to take it in.

"You mean—we just give up?" Kat asked tremulously.

Andy tried to pull himself together. "No. I . . . Maybe I'll think of something in the morning."

The morning began with the delivery of the *Oregonian*. Mr. Buckle came in from the mailbox unrolling it, stopped in the kitchen doorway to read an item in the left lower corner of the front page, then tossed it onto the breakfast table, remarking, "Well, no need to avoid that party line now. You can phone your mom from here, twins."

Kat snatched the paper and monopolized it before Andy could put down his milk glass. He had to read over her left shoulder; Mrs. Buckle abandoned a griddle full of pancakes to lean over the right one. The article was as informative as yesterday's *Oregonian* reporter could make it, considering that he had almost no information to impart. County authorities were investigating Monday after a human skeleton, probably a small boy's, had been found by two children. . . . The children were not named. The rock *was* named, identified as an old landmark on the farm of H. C. Buckle near Harper's Mill. Dr. James Hutton, county medical examiner, was busy conducting tests. Buckle, well-known breeder of Belgian draft horses, had stated . . . very little, it turned out, beyond his name and occupation. Sheriff's Officer Cameron had had no comment at this time. Andy felt almost sorry for the reporter, who had been hard-pressed to achieve two paragraphs.

Mrs. Buckle went back to her griddle, predicting darkly, "We're gonna have sightseers all over this place, or I'm a cross-eyed pygmy."

In the end the twins had to walk up to the Lodge after all to use the phone. Obviously Mr. Sweet had kept his promise to see Len Harper before he left for work. Just as obviously, Mrs. Len Harper had heard the whole conversation ("listening behind the door!" Kat said darkly) and hurried down to open the supermarket, take her place behind the cash register, and begin dispensing the story to all comers along with their change. The Buckles' party line was tied up for an hour as everybody in Harper's Mill called everybody else—including the Buckles—to ask if they'd seen the morning paper and if they'd been to the store yet. Mrs. Buckle finally settled herself by the kitchen phone with some busywork and resigned her morning to barking "Hal-lo"s and discouraging curiosity.

Dodie was still in outer space or somewhere. The phone rang and rang. By the time Andy and Kat gave up and headed back down the lane, they met the first townsfolk heading up it, toward the rock, and they reached the Buckles' to find the phone there still jammed with discussion of the most interesting news to hit the area since the eruption of Mount St. Helens. The discussers were begin-

ning to take sides. Mrs. Buckle, calculating expertly
on the basis of one ten-party line and her sister's
bulletins reporting from another, estimated ten
percent for and sixty percent against opening any
grave for any reason at any time, with another
twenty percent considering an exception in this
case and the rest undecided. The thirty percent in
favor were now dividing on whether the Sweets
or the Historical Society should have the say.

"It's none of their business *anyway*," muttered
Kat as she and Andy wandered out of the house to
sit on the front steps, feeling at loose ends, and by
now as worried about Dodie as about the growing
commotion in Harper's Mill.

"I knew we shouldn't have told anybody!" Andy
said. "I knew it all along. We should've *kept still*,
until we figured out what to do ourselves."

Kat, reversing their usual roles, told him not to
be silly. "We couldn't keep still once we'd found
him! You know we couldn't."

Andy knew it. But he was almost in despair, and
the longer the day went on the more desperate he
felt. Everything was out of hand; nothing was turning out right, and there wasn't a thing he could do
about it. The sightseers kept coming—not just
neighbors now but strangers from nearly as far
away as Portland, who evidently had nothing
better to do, once they'd seen the morning paper,
than jump right in their cars and head for the

Buckles' lane. They all brought cameras; a few brought little kids or yappy little dogs. A cloud of dust hung over the lane, and the parking space in front of the old graveyard was crowded. Len Harper's sanctimonious pronouncements around town about "heathenish goings-on" and "disturbing the dead"—accurately predicted by Aunt Henry—were influencing the percentages, according to Mrs. Buckle's party-line poll. So was Mrs. Len's talkative presence behind the cash register. Nobody on the other side seemed to be talking back. Even Mr. Buckle, chagrined and illogically feeling it was all his fault, tended to wander off to the barn alone and stay with the horses. Ellerton was helping the beleaguered sheriff's deputy guard "the Site."

To Andy, it seemed that Jacob himself—*their* Jacob—was lost in the uproar, forgotten by everybody but him and Kat.

Around four o'clock Officer Cameron managed to break through the party-line blockade to inform Mr. Buckle that the medical examiner had now certified "the evidence" as much too old to indicate a crime by anybody now alive. ("Which we already knew," muttered Andy.) He had then contacted the University's archaeological department, but the bones weren't old *enough* to interest them.

"So—?" prompted Andy anxiously.

"So sheriff's office is withdrawing from the case. I'm supposed to tell their man to go on home."

"But what about the—what about Jacob?"

"The evidence will remain in the evidence property room until claimed," quoted Mr. Buckle dryly. "And the sooner the better, I gather. Cameron kinda hinted they need the space."

"What if it's *not* claimed? Would it just be— thrown out?"

"No, no, son, they'd bury the bones decent. I dunno just where."

Not in his own bed, though. It wasn't good enough. It wasn't *right*.

Kat said rather wildly, "But who's going to claim him?"

"I guess that's not Cameron's problem."

"Well, he's leavin' *us* one," Mrs. Buckle retorted. "When that sheriff's fella goes, there's gonna be nobody but Ellerton up there to cope with all those rubberneckers! And more and more'll come—"

"No, that won't happen," Mr. Buckle told her firmly.

He strode out of the kitchen and up the lane. A few minutes later the first of the sightseer's cars rolled reluctantly down it toward the county road. The others followed in a dust-raising line. The sheriff's man brought up the rear, stopped to let Mr. Buckle and Ellerton out at the house, and departed. The two of them went into the barn and emerged bearing a length of heavy chain, two four-foot iron stakes, and a sign reading *Private Prop-*

erty. No Hunting. No Trespassing. They got into Mr. Buckle's car and drove in their turn down the lane.

Mrs. Buckle gave a dry little laugh and turned away from the window. "Little early for pheasant season. But we won't have any more sightseers, you can bet your best bridle on that. They're gonna block the lane."

Shortly afterwards, the twins crunched along side by side up the graveled lane, heading for home. The dust still hung invisibly over the familiar route, tickling their nostrils as it settled over weeds and hazel leaves in a gauzy pall that dimmed everything to olive drab. Both glanced sadly toward the rock as they came even with it; both stopped in their tracks with gasps of disgust.

"Boy! People sure are slobs!" Andy growled.

Without further discussion they climbed up the trampled bank and began picking up the litter that desecrated the little clearing around the rock. "The evidence" might be gone, but this had been Jacob's place for over a hundred years, and in Andy's mind it still was. Stubbornly he gathered used matches, ground-out cigarette stubs and their crumpled packages, candy wrappers, little wads of Kleenex, a popsicle stick or two. There was even a half-empty potato chip sack, in which a blue jay was taking an interest.

"Where are the dog-food cans?" inquired Kat coldly as she sent the jay flying and stuffed her trash into the potato chip sack. "They brought dogs, too."

"I guess we ought to be glad they didn't bring their camping gear," Andy muttered. He had found a discarded plastic bag to hold his unattractive gleanings, and he took a last look around as he knotted its top. Except for the scuffed dirt and broken ferns—which a little time would mend—the place again looked its old sun-filled, lonely self. Lonelier than ever—now that they knew what was gone.

Kat spoke wistfully at his elbow. "I don't suppose he'll ever come back now. I mean—I guess he can't."

Andy wasn't sure if the removal of "the evidence" meant the end of Jacob—at least here by the rock. He didn't know the rules for ghosts. He only knew he'd failed the one that had appealed to him—failed him miserably—and sentenced him to what must be worse than before. Now he couldn't even tell him he was sorry. Because the trouble with Jacob . . . Andy heaved a sigh that seemed to start at his shoe tops. Maybe nobody could ever unravel the trouble with Jacob.

"I wish I could at least explain," he said to Kat. "D'you suppose he knows what happened?"

He must know *something* did. Maybe not what."
Kat tugged at Andy's sleeve. "Come on. Let's go."

Reluctantly Andy followed her, so heavy with discouragement that it felt as if he were uprooting each foot before he moved it. At the top of the bank he paused for one last glance back, and almost did take root.

Jacob was standing there by the rock, on the same side as the empty cave—a much dimmer and less substantial little towhead, looking somehow remote but wearier than ever.

"Oh, Andy . . . ," breathed Kat, at his elbow.

"Jacob, listen—" Andy croaked, and had to swallow and clear his throat. "Jacob, I'm sorry, I tried, we both did, honest! It just—got away from us. . . ."

He explained as well as he could, but quickly, because it didn't seem as if they had very long. And he was right; Jacob listened resignedly a minute or two, but before Andy had finished he wandered away into the trees and was gone. There was absolutely no use trying to call him back, now or ever again, Andy was sure of it.

Kat broke the long, quivering silence. "Andy, I don't think he blames us. I think he expected it."

"He's probably used to it," said Andy sadly. "After all, he's been trying to get back in bed for over a hundred years. Imagine!"

They exchanged a wincing stare, trying to imagine.

"I hope somebody helps him, sometime." Kat suddenly looked appalled. "Andy! *Can* anybody, now, with the—'evidence'—gone?"

For a terrible instant Andy felt as if he were dropping feet first into permanent gloom. Then he found himself rebelling against it—resisting, refusing to go on feeling like such a wimp. *"We're* going to. We're going to keep right on trying." He could feel himself losing his temper, and it was like a shot of adrenalin mixed with common sense. Indignantly he shook off the unfamiliar weight of despair. "I'll tell you one thing, he's not going to wait another hundred years—or even another week —not if I have to open that grave myself!"

"Yourself? What are you *talking* about?"

"Well, I wouldn't be scared to start digging." Andy plunged down the bank to the path, feeling practically invincible—like Superman. It was a great sensation. "You and I both know there's nothing scary under that clover! No bones. We already found the bones."

"But there might be others! Somebody else's," Kat said rather breathlessly as they started the climb up the hill.

"There can't be. That wouldn't make sense—to just swap one body for another one. Would it?"

"Not unless you'd murdered the second one."
Kat was beginning to sound strained and scared
again.

"Then you could just wall *it* up under the rock.
No, it's something else." Andy stopped to catch
his breath and ponder, bracing himself against a
tree. "Why would anybody dig up a grave?" he
asked, more or less rhetorically.

Kat answered prosaically. "To take out the
body." She shivered. "They must've wanted it
awful bad."

"Well, they didn't! They didn't want Jacob at
all—they just stuck him away in the closest spot
they could find."

"To steal something, then?" Kat hazarded.

"Steal what? Shoe buttons? What would he
have—that little kid in his coffin—that anybody'd
want?"

"Well—a ring or something . . ."

"No, what they wanted was the *grave*. But what
for?"

"To hide something in. Maybe something valuable?" Kat said with sudden interest.

"Kat, don't get going again on the family jewels!
What good would valuables be to anybody if they
were stuck away in a grave?"

Reluctantly, Kat ceded the point. "Not something valuable. Then—something awful?"

They climbed on slowly. Andy had a feeling the

whole business might get clearer if he could just see back around a couple of corners—or if the picture didn't keep dissolving just when he thought he'd got it into focus.

"We need somebody to help us think," Kat said impatiently. "My brain keeps going all gooey."

"I wonder where Dodie is." Andy sighed as he unlocked the cottage.

He went straight to the phone and dialed the familiar number, and listened to the all-too-familiar repeated rings. After eight or nine of them he banged the phone onto its hook, then suddenly listened.

"What's that?" Kat exclaimed at the same moment.

But they both knew it was a car door slamming —this time the blessedly familiar *ka-blonk* of Dodie's aging Pontiac. They collided in their rush out of the kitchen, took flying leaps down the back steps and all but knocked the breath out of Dodie, who was rushing full tilt toward them.

Kat burst into tears and clung. "Where've you been? Where've you *been*? We've been so *worried!*"

"Where have *I* been? Where have *you*? And what does this *mean*?" Dodie wrenched open her purse and produced a torn scrap of newspaper, which she waved in their faces. Andy knew what it was without looking—the *Oregonian* article.

"We've been *trying* to call you! But the phone just rang and rang and—"

"Oh murder, I forgot. Of course it did. You pathetic orphans, did you think I'd run off with the roofing man? I was at the hospital—"

"*Hospital?*" chorused her children.

"Relax. Great-Aunt Madge had surgery yesterday—scared to death, poor old dear, and nobody to be with her."

"Is she okay?" asked Andy, instantly alarmed. He liked Great-Aunt Madge.

"She is now. No thanks to my cousin Florrie—who is absolutely *useless* in a crisis," added Dodie. Having got that off her chest, she demanded why they were discussing all this in the middle of the driveway, and herded them into the house.

Dodie's two-day disappearance was prosaically unmysterious once she explained it. The moment she got the news about Great-Aunt Madge, she'd gone directly to the nursing home and ended by staying through the dinner hour. "I only went home to sleep—and then got up at the crack, of course, to take the old dear to the hospital. I did try to call you last night, but *this* phone just rang and rang—"

"We stayed at Mr. Buckle's," Kat told her.

"Well, I thought of that. But by then it was too late to disturb the Buckles. . . . I didn't see *this* till I left the hospital this afternoon." Dodie waved the

clipping again. "These anonymous 'neighbor children'—?"

"That was us," Andy said.

"I knew it. I *knew* it. I must have E.S.P. I had this
overwhelming presentiment. . . . Of course then I
did phone the Buckles, but *their* line was busy, and
no wonder. Did you actually—unearth—some poor
child's skeleton?"

"Yeah. But it wasn't as awful as you're thinking,
Dodie."

"It was, too," said Kat. "Just at first."

"But . . . Andy, *tell* me."

Andy swallowed. The moment had come, and it
was just as difficult as he'd suspected. "Dodie—
this'll sound pretty weird, but—do you believe in
ghosts?"

Dodie gave him a stare of surprise which quickly
changed to exasperation. "*Mon petit chou*, don't
change the subject!"

"That is the subject," Andy said hastily. When
Dodie called you her little cabbage it was time to
talk fast and make sense, but he tried once more.
"I just wish you'd—tell us your views."

"And I wish you'd get on with your story."

So Andy sighed and started from the beginning.

CHAPTER SEVENTEEN

O ne thing about Dodie—when you told her something, she listened. Frequently she even heard things you hadn't meant to go into and weren't sure you'd said. She absorbed Andy's story in silence, without interruption, and looked at the shoe button for quite a while.

Finally she said, "I see why you asked me for my views on ghosts."

"Personally I still don't believe in 'em," Andy told her defiantly. "Except for Jacob."

"Do you, Dodie?" Kat asked.

"Kat, my darling idiot, you've known me all your life—answer the question yourself."

"You don't."

"Of course I don't. However, that doesn't mean there aren't any. I don't pretend to *know* one way or the other." As her children gaped at this unusual statement, she added impatiently, "There's a lot I don't know—probably even a few things about French verb endings. Certainly about ghosts."

"But what besides ghosts?" asked Andy, who did not believe the part about French verb endings.

"Well—take quarks. I am totally ignorant about quarks."

"Quarks?" Kat echoed in bewilderment.

"Oh, please, not quarks!" Andy begged. "Phil Darling talks about stuff like that all the time, and he doesn't even know what they are—he admits it!"

"Not even the physicists know exactly what they are," Dodie informed him.

"Okay! So why bother—"

"Don't they *really*?" Kat cut in.

"Really," Dodie assured her. "They don't even know for sure quarks exist—only that something of the sort *must* exist or certain things that happen wouldn't keep happening, if you follow me."

Kat turned to Andy in triumph. "There! Isn't that just what I've been saying about Jacob all along?"

Andy leaped to his feet and took a turn around the kitchen. "All we do is jabber. I want to do something! And I want help!"

Dodie stood up, too, reaching for an apron. "You've got it," she told him. "Kat, find me a can of tuna fish, we're all starving. While I fix food, tell me what you want me to do."

Andy studied her hopefully. "You mean you believe in Jacob after all? You think we oughta—"

"Andy, my views on ghosts are irrelevant. I

believe in you two, and that if you say something peculiar happened, something did. And that it's not a major sin to open a grave in the hope of righting a wrong—providing the authorities consent. I'm behind you all the way."

"Oh, *Dodie!*" Kat gasped, and flung her arms around her, including the bread and bread knife she was holding.

By the time this small crisis had been resolved without bloodshed, Andy had enjoyed an inward leap of relief and then hauled himself swiftly back to earth.

"That's our problem—the authorities consenting," he reminded Dodie.

"Meaning Mr. Len Harper?"

"Not just him, now. The whole town."

"He keeps blabbing. And *lobbying*," Kat said darkly.

"The town is not the proper authority," Dodie pointed out.

"No, he thinks *he* is. But he's not the whole Historical Society, only the president. And the Sweets are *sort of* living descendants, and everybody likes them better than him, so—"

"So he lobbies. Andy, pour some milk. Isn't Mr. Buckle on your side?"

"Oh, sure! But he's got to keep a low profile, so as not to make things worse. We need somebody *official,"* Andy fretted as he reached down the glasses. "But the bones are too old for the sheriff to bother with. And too new for the archaeologists."

"And not a soul but Aunt Henry believes in your little ghost?"

"Nobody but Mr. Buckle. And I think— Dawnelle," said Kat.

"The others just think we're making that part up," Andy added indignantly. "I knew we'd be better off if we'd never told anybody about Jacob! But how else could we convince people? Jacob was why we went to look for the grave in the first place. And why we were digging around the—"

"Wait!" commanded Dodie, standing motionless with a fork in one hand and the olive jar in the other. "I think you just passed your most important question."

Andy stared, thought back, and located it. "How else could we convince people?" he said slowly.

"Yes. Leaving out the ghost." Dodie began to chop olives for the sandwich mix. "Kat, put some potato chips in that wooden bowl. Andy, get out the plates. If it's the ghost that's in your way, we'll have to go some other route."

"But what other—"

"Concentrate on the skeleton instead. Everybody believes in that. And nobody believes it ever belonged where it was found."

"But if the sheriff's not interested in the skeleton
—or the archaeologists either—" Kat waved her
arms. "Who does that leave?"

"The historians," said Dodie.

After a startled silence, Andy banged the stack
of plates down onto the table with a triumphant
clash. "You mean go over Mr. Harper's head!
Tackle the Historical Society members! Do some
lobbying ourselves!"

Kat exclaimed, "Oh, Dodie, that might be a great
idea! That nice postmaster's a member—and Mrs.
Corey-who-cooks—"

Dodie showed no inclination to dance gleefully
around the kitchen. "It'll take more than lobbying
to get that Society interested in tearing up one of
their graves. What I had in mind was supporting
evidence—or even proof."

The excitement subsided. "How do we get that?"
Kat said doubtfully.

"First, we eat," Dodie told her, plunking the
plate of sandwiches down on the table. "Then,
before it gets dark, I want to see for myself that
cave and that rock and that pathetic little grave.
After that, we use our heads."

There was still plenty of pale summer-evening
light when they helped Dodie down the last jump
to the cow path. Attempted to help her; she
managed with careless agility on her own. Thirty-

eight wasn't actually old, Andy knew that—but when a person was your own parent, you forgot.

He discovered he felt strange, walking with Dodie along this path that was so specially his and Kat's—strange and a little edgy, as though maybe he shouldn't be doing it. It was *him* Jacob had appealed to. Nobody else could care so much. Kat had no such problems; she was behaving like a sunflower finally locating the sun.

Dodie seemed as casual as if this were an ordinary evening's stroll; but when she stood with them at the far side of Beaver Rock and looked around the lonely clearing, toward the fringe of woods where Jacob had so often shown himself, then down at the low, dark cleft that was the cave, her silence, and the slight tenseness around her mouth, was enough to ease Andy's mind a little.

"So this is the scene of the crime," she said in a tone obviously intended to be light, but which came out flat and quiet.

"Well—we're not saying there was a *crime*," Kat objected. "Jacob wasn't murdered, he died of diphtheria."

"It was a crime to move him from his grave!" Andy said.

"Oh, *yes*. That was."

"Imagine. A little nine-year-old," said Dodie. She drew a long breath. "Why, oh why, would anybody do such a thing?"

"To take out the body," Kat reminded her with a weary flap of her hand. "To steal something. To hide something valuable or awful."

"Or something incriminating?" Dodie suggested.

Andy looked at her with interest. "That's a new answer! Best one so far."

"Why?" demanded Kat.

"Well, because! Look—say you've got something that connects you to a crime—"

"What kind of something?"

"*I* dunno, I just thought of this. But if the law's right on your heels, and you've gotta hide this thing fast, you wouldn't think twice about digging up a grave!"

As Kat paused, evidently trying to picture herself in the role of criminal, Dodie said, "I want to see that grave. Come on, before the light goes."

Andy led the way back down the bank, along the grassy way to the gates of the cemetery, and over the mattress of clover to the small, weathered column in the far corner. He pulled aside the trailing brambles.

JACOB SAMUEL SWEET

Apr. 16, 1867–Feb. 4, 1876

R.I.P.

Beloved child

Dodie looked in silence, her expression hard to read. But her jaw was beginning to get its squarish

look, Andy noticed with satisfaction. A little after-
sunset breeze ruffled everybody's hair and played a
moment with the brambles, then subsided. Dodie
turned away. The sky arching over the pasture was
opal, shading to topaz in the west, as they closed
the iron gates and headed home.

Dodie suddenly burst out, "Why a *grave*, speci-
fically? I find the very idea an outrage. And it seems
such a chancy thing to do! If anybody saw you . . .
Why not just dig a hole?"

"Somebody'd wonder why—unless you dug it in
your own garden," Andy said. "And it was winter
—no gardens. A fresh-dug hole is always kind of
suspicious, isn't it? But not a fresh-dug grave." He
wondered if that was true, really. Dodie looked
unconvinced. Actually, so was he.

Kat was still imagining herself a criminal. "Why
should I dig at all? Why couldn't I just put whatever it was under the rock? It hid Jacob all those
years."

That stopped Andy. But only for a moment.
"The thing might've been too big. Or the wrong
shape to fit in under there. That place is awful low
and flat."

"So what's high and lumpy and incriminating?"
Kat asked vaguely.

"But not too big to fit in a coffin," Dodie put in.
"The coffin must still be in the grave."

"Yes, I suppose . . . Well, if we could figure all that out . . . Why did you say 'winter'? We don't know when it happened."

"Well—Jacob died in winter. February fourth, don't you *remember*?" Andy doubted if he'd ever forget those weathered dates. Out of the corner of his eye he glimpsed Dodie studying him, but she said nothing. He went on. "The way I see it, there's got to've been some kind of crime, committed around here somewhere, just a few days after Jacob died."

"Why just a few days?" Kat argued. "That only makes it harder. We could allow a month or two.

"No," Andy said stubbornly. "The grave would have to be fresh. Then nobody'd notice if it'd been tampered with—not if it was all smoothed out afterwards just the way the real gravediggers had left it." As they abandoned the path and started the steep trudge up the hillside, he warmed to his theory, which was only forming as he talked. "Look—if you wanted to hide incriminating stuff in a grave, would you be fool enough to start digging through all that mat of clover back there? You might as well put up a sign saying, 'X marks the spot.' You'd never get an *old* grave back to looking right!" He stopped at the edge of the woods, out of breath from arguing while climbing, and glanced hopefully at his mother.

She only said, "But why a grave at all? That has me stumped."

Andy took a last brooding look at the pearly sky behind them, then started the final climb. It stumped him, too. He tried to visualize some bad guy of 1876, running from the posse or whatever, realizing he'd never make it and had better dump— dump what? Something high, lumpy, and incriminating—but not valuable because what good would it be to him buried? And deciding, of all places, on a grave. Because . . .

"*I* know why!" Andy exclaimed. He turned, as they reached the cottage clearing, and stared at the others.

"You know why what?" Kat asked.

"Why he picked a grave—Jacob's grave—to hide stuff in! *He saw it*! That's got to be it. He was right there, down on that path by the cemetery, running away, and in a panic, and he *saw* that fresh grave. It gave him the idea."

"And he just happened to have a shovel. . . ." Kat muttered.

"Wait, let him finish," Dodie told her, opening the door.

Andy followed them into the kitchen, his brain still racing. "Well, he could've found a shovel! He could've *stolen* one. There might've been two guys, not just one—and they might've had a *little* time— maybe all night. So he dug up that fresh dirt, made the transfer, shoved Jacob in under that rock and stuffed some rocks in the opening—" Andy stopped.

"And thought he was safe," Dodie said. She put her hands on Andy's shoulders and sat him down on a chair. "And I guess he was."

"Yes!" Kat said, wide-eyed and abruptly converted. "Because nobody'd guess. *Usually* nobody ever disturbs a grave."

"What's more," Andy said slowly, "a grave is *marked*. You could go away for maybe years and years, and always find it again when you were ready. Those guys meant to come back!"

The three of them looked at each other. Dodie said, "I think we're getting very warm."

"Are we?" Kat said anxiously. "Can you think of anything that's high, and lumpy, and incriminating, that you'd want to hide for maybe years and years and then come back for?"

"Yes. I can," Andy told her, and he suddenly knew he had it. "A big box of *loot*. It *was* valuable, Kat. They didn't rob Jacob—they robbed somebody else!"

"Bingo," said Dodie softly.

For a moment his family contemplated Andy with an admiration he wholeheartedly shared. If anything, he was more impressed than they—and much more surprised. "Do you suppose that's really it?" he asked with sudden doubt.

"I don't see why not—everything fits," Kat said. "But we won't know unless they open the grave."

Right back where they started. Andy refused to stay there. "We'll find out stuff about old crimes! We can look up something somewhere—can't we, Dodie? Where do we look, the library?"

"Not the library." Dodie kicked off her shoes and padded around switching on lamps. "We look in the files of the Oregon Historical Society in Portland. They have old newspaper clippings, letters, affidavits, eyewitness accounts, everything you can think of. *I* look. Tomorrow when I go back to town."

"You're going right back to Portland?" Kat exclaimed in dismay.

"Have I got an option? Somebody's got to do this criminological research. I'd have to go anyway. Mr. Handy'll be finished and want to tell me all about gutters and downspouts and things. Now listen. Sit down at that table, you two detectives. I want a list. Of everything, every single tiny detail, that you know *for sure* about the rock, the grave, and the real little Jacob Sweet who died of diphtheria. No theories, and nothing about the ghost. Right now, before we go to bed."

It was a pretty long list by the time they finished. But Andy lay awake for some time, picking it over in his mind, mentally deleting such irrelevant items as Aunt Henry's Prince of Romania and the spilled coffee, then uncertainly putting them back.

He read the list through next morning after Dodie was already in the car, scouring his memory again. Dodie flapped her hand out the car window. "Just give it to me, Andy, I want to get going. I'll phone at noon." She plucked the list from his hand and was off.

"What do we do now?" Kat asked as they watched the small dust cloud disappear toward Hidden Creek Road.

"Nothing *to* do. Just wait."

CHAPTER EIGHTEEN

It was the hardest possible assignment—harder than splitting kindling. Andy did that, too, for an hour or so, while Kat silently practiced Czerny, then fetched and carried for Mrs. Corey, who was making pies for the freezer. At ten o'clock, feeling as if they'd been waiting a week already, they braved Harper's Mill to get groceries and pick up the mail.

As they had suspected, they were now famous— or more accurately, notorious—as the kids who'd stumbled on some old bones and told the sheriff's man a ghost story and were now trying to get decent folks to dig up a grave. That was the Len Harper contingent's point of view, and whether the comments were scandalized or merely amused, they were discomforting if you were the target. The pro-Jacob minority party—the nice postmaster was one—didn't have nearly as much to say.

"*Somebody* could stick up for us!" Kat said indignantly as she stalked beside Andy back along the county road.

"Sensible people don't carry on like guinea

hens," Andy told her, though he had private doubts about the motives of some of their supporters.

"No," Kat agreed. "They don't make up their minds in the first five minutes, either. They wait and see. And it'll be worth waiting for—because they're going to see!"

Andy hoped she was right. It all depended on what, if anything, Dodie could find. He glanced at his watch. Still an hour and seventeen minutes before she would phone. "Let's stop in at the Buckles'," he suggested. "They don't even know Dodie finally showed up."

"Oh, let's do! I want to know what Mr. Buckle thinks of our detective work." Kat added hopefully, "He might have some more ideas."

Mr. Buckle, whom they found in the barn shampooing Bonnie's tail, was startled, then impressed, by their deductions, though he had no fresh ideas to add, and after a moment's thought cautioned them not to count on a speedy victory, no matter what Dodie found.

"I hate to be a clammy blanket," he apologized. "But I know this town. If there'd been any mysterious crime committed around here, even in eighteen seventy-six, folks'd still be airing their theories about it and taking sides. That's not saying there've been no crimes—but the criminals've all been caught and locked up, far as I ever heard."

"There *could* have been one nobody heard about," Kat insisted.

"Oh, sure, there could," he agreed comfortingly, but not, Andy thought, very convincingly. He rinsed the pale cascade of horsehair in a bucket, then picked up an old bath towel and began briskly rubbing it dry, while Bonnie philosophically reached for another mouthful of hay. After a moment he went on, "I've been trying, myself, to think how to work more folks around to our point of view—without opening my big mouth and riling Len."

"*Some* of 'em are on our side," Andy reminded him.

"About thirty percent, Myra's sister's estimating now," Mr. Buckle said dryly.

"And half of those for the wrong reasons," Kat said. "Like that Mrs. Jenkins in the stamp line, Andy—did it seem to you she didn't really care about Jacob—or right or wrong—but just wanted . . . to watch somebody open a grave?"

"Yeah. Just because it might be gruesome." It was exactly what had occurred to him.

Mr. Buckle said, "You're always gonna find sensation seekers—like all those folks trampling around here yesterday. But don't knock 'em, Kat honey. We might end up needing their vote."

It was a dismal thought. Andy sighed. "I wish it

was over, that's all. I wish it was already next summer! Then it'd all be behind us and we could just be having a great time driving Bonnie and Clyde and being *normal*."

"Well, we still got half of this summer left. Let's drive a little while right now," Mr. Buckle suggested.

"With Bonnie's tail all wet?" Kat protested.

Mr. Buckle laughed and said Bonnie didn't catch cold easily, and the sun would help dry it. "Clyde's is already pretty well aired out—I did him first. Let's use 'em both. You go fetch the light team harness, and Andy and I'll pull out the Jersey buggy, and we'll get these two lazybones out of here for a little honest work."

It was a wonderful relief to be starting up the lane again behind the two bobbing rumps with their shining clean tails, just as if there weren't a care or problem in your world. Andy drove first, keeping his eyes resolutely straight ahead as they rolled past the rock and along the grassy way in front of the cemetery.

Once in the pasture and trotting breezily beside its fencerow, they all relaxed, and Mr. Buckle reverted to the remark Andy had made in the barn. "Do I take it you're coming back here next summer?"

"Oh—I just said that. I don't know. I guess not.

Uncle Richard won't need us to run the Lodge. I wish I could, though," Andy added, suddenly realizing just how much he did wish it. He took a deep, savoring breath of country air, in which he could sort out the scents of grass and sun-dried weeds and horses and Ivory soap and the buggy's old leather, spiced with a whiff of firs from the wooded hill. "I *would*, in a minute, if Uncle Richard'd let me stay with him. And if I could find a job. D'you think I could? At home I always mow lawns."

"Not many honest-to-goodness lawns around these farmhouses," Mr. Buckle said. "But I might could use a stable boy, if you're interested."

"*Interested?*" Andy echoed, nearly dropping the reins in his excitement. He hastily reestablished his hot line to the horses' mouths. "D'you think I know enough about it?"

"Doesn't take much know-how to clean stables —just willing muscle. You've got a real feel for horses and driving—I'd like to help you develop it. Anyway, I always need summer help. Generally got two or three shows—there's one coming up in Salem coupla weeks from now—and later the county fairs—it's work. You could put up at our place. Myra'd like it. You and Kat both, if you want."

"I'll probably be going to music camp next July,"

Kat said—but not as quickly as she would have once, Andy noticed. She, too, had put down some roots in the Hidden Creek countryside and the Buckles' barn. She added, "Maybe I could come in August. If that's okay?"

"Fine! We'll sound out your mama, first chance we get," Mr. Buckle told them with what sounded flatteringly like real pleasure.

Andy got no chance to bask in it; the mention of Dodie brought him back with a thud to this summer, and the angle of the sun, which was climbing fast toward noon. Kat, too, frowned and looked at her watch.

"Let me drive, Andy. We've only got twenty minutes before Dodie phones."

It turned out to be nearer two hours, every minute harder to get through than the last one. The twins stayed right in the cottage, hovering near the phone, staring and sometimes glaring at it, willing it to ring.

At last it did. Kat was nearest, and snatched it. "Dodie? Well, *hey*, you said noon, and here it is nearly . . . You *did*?" She fell silent, listening tensely, while Andy, tenser still, hovered behind her. Suddenly her hand reached for the notepad on the counter, then scrabbled in a drawer. She hissed, "*Pencil!*" Andy found one, watched her scrawl "Buck, Sw, El, H, Off Cam, crm afall, L 7, shrf t chrg," then toss the pencil down, and after a final "okay—g'bye," hang up. Looking a little dazed, she turned to him.

"Well?" he demanded.

"She found something," Kat said. "I don't know what."

"You don't *know*? Why didn't you *ask* her?"

"She didn't give me a chance! She just said she'd got what looked very much like the goods, and she'd be here with it by dinnertime, and we're to tell Mr. Buckle and the Sweets and Ellerton—" Kat reached for her scrawled note—" and the Harpers, and call Officer Cameron to say there may have been a crime after all, and would he like to come up to the Lodge this evening, too, and hear about it, in case the sheriff's office should take charge. About seven o'clock." She tossed the note onto the counter. "That's all I know."

Andy rolled his eyes. "I wish I'd answered the phone!"

"Well, she wouldn't have told you anything more. She was overparked." Kat picked up the note again. "We'd better get at it—let's go see Mr. Buckle first. He'll call the sheriff."

Mr. Buckle started up from a porch chair as they turned into the barnyard, and came to meet them. He listened to their news with an interest only slightly tinged with doubt. "She sounded pretty confident, did she?" he asked Kat.

"She sounded sure!"

"You called Officer Cameron yet?"

"We sort of hoped you'd come up to the Lodge and do it for us."

"And I was hoping you'd say that," admitted Mr. Buckle. But instead of starting toward the car he turned and stared off across his hilly acres a minute, an odd little gleam in his eyes. "Are you kids gamblers?" he inquired.

Kat said blankly, "I don't know. Depends."

"We'd risk anything for Jacob, if that's what you mean," Andy assured him.

"Well, I used to be a pretty good poker player. Come on in the house."

Mystified, they followed him into the kitchen. But they were mystified no longer when he picked up the phone, calmly waited for the clicks of nine other lifted receivers, then called Harpers, Sweets, and the sheriff's office on his party line.

Dodie drove in, tired and uncommunicative, at about four-thirty. Andy and Kat met her with a bombardment of questions at which she flapped both hands as if fending off flies and pushed past them into the house, where she paused long enough to rummage in her purse and produce a Xeroxed page. She handed this to Andy, said, "I'm going to take a *long, relaxing* bath and I don't want any questions shouted through the door." She then disappeared into her bedroom.

Andy stared at the sheet of paper in his hands, said, "Hey, look out," as Kat jolted his elbow trying to see, and finally focused on the print in front of him. It was part of a newspaper page—as large a rectangle as the Xerox machine would handle—with no dateline or beginning or headline or anything else to tell him what it was all about, but it seemed to be a lot of short articles, and everywhere he looked he kept seeing "Umatilla." Umatilla County. East from Umatilla. Wells-Fargo express to Umatilla. And there was a "Pendleton." All those places were in Eastern Oregon—clear on the other side of the Cascade Mountains and some of them nearly to the Blues. Nothing to do with Harper's Mill at all.

"But *Dodie*—!" he protested, heading for the closed bedroom door.

"Read it!" came the muffled command. "Third item down—I've got it marked."

Kat was beside him, grabbing at the paper, jabbing a finger at the place. "There. The city of The Dalles. That's closer . . . *January 30?* But Dodie! Jacob didn't even die till—"

"*Mes petits choux, read* it!" yelled their mother, and turned on the bath.

The twins carried the paper to the kitchen table, sat down, and read it through. When they finished, they slowly raised their heads and stared thoughtfully into space.

"Thirty days hath September," Kat began. "April, June—"

"January's got thirty-one," Andy told her. "That's Phil's birthday. "And they *weren't* driving along a highway in a car, you know."

"Horses?" Kat hazarded.

"Maybe even on foot. There'd've been snow, bad weather. It could've easily taken several days."

"But what if they went by river boat? If there *were* any boats on the Columbia, taking passengers —and going regular."

"And in midwinter," Andy added. "I'll bet there weren't."

They looked at each other, then once more studied the paper—the all-important support for their reasoned theory. If only, thought Andy, it didn't have so many holes.

CHAPTER NINETEEN

The effect of Mr. Buckle's gamble was precisely as expected: His hand was called. In addition to Officer Cameron, the Buckle family, and the Sweets and Harpers, half the town turned up at the Lodge that evening to see what cards he was holding—or knew the Petersons to be holding.

"It's only the Historical Society Executive Committee—and Reverend Mahaffey—and a few others," Mr. Buckle told the twins in a reassuring whisper as they stood rigid with stage fright, watching people wander half hesitantly, half defiantly, into the big lounge. The Lodge was, after all, a public building, their faces said—and they were the public.

"There come Ned and Maria Jenkins," said Mrs. Buckle dryly. "They're always the last ones anywhere. Now we can get started."

Andy hoped so. As the Buckles found a couple of unoccupied chairs near Ellerton, he glanced toward the glass-partitioned office, where Dodie had been talking to Officer Cameron while people straggled in, and wondered if he should go tell her about all the gate-crashers. He did a head count. Only four-

teen extra altogether, besides the eleven actually
invited—but it still looked like half the town. Just
then Dodie looked at her watch and turned around.
For an instant she gaped at the unexpected crowd,
then got her Campion Hall "formidable lady" face
on, marched to the main door and locked it, and
turned off the outside lights. Andy slipped hurriedly around the edge of the room and joined her
in the entry.

"Andy! Where did we get this *audience*?" she
hissed at him.

"Party line," said Andy. He darted a glance at
Officer Cameron, who was just emerging from the
office, and lowered his voice to a mumble. "I think
Mr. Buckle thought they might as well hear first-
hand. About the 'goods' you said you'd got. Kat
and I told him you sounded sure, so he's—got a lot
of faith in it."

"And now you're not so sure yourself," said
Dodie.

Andy swallowed. "There's a lot of ifs. But it's
worth the gamble." Anything is, for Jacob, he reminded himself as he rejoined Kat by the big
windows. But he hoped he wasn't going to let Mr.
Buckle down with an awful crash. Or anybody
else on their side. He couldn't help looking toward
the big couch at the right of the fireplace where
Martin Sweet's family—all but Aunt Henry, who

was at home in bed—were sitting like statues in a row. He found Dawnelle watching him, with a determined, don't-worry-about-a-thing expression. But she didn't know about all the ifs.

Dodie walked straight to the fireplace, turned to face the grouping of couches and armchairs as if it were a classroom, and remarked bluntly that she hadn't expected to address a crowd, but she supposed it was just as well.

"As you know," she began, "my children and I are newcomers to this neighorhood. My son Andy had a very strange introduction to the place."

She told them briefly, keeping it simple, about the Jacob-sightings, then went on to his and Kat's search for—and discovery of—the grave and the tintype image of a nine-year-old named Jacob Sweet of whom their only knowledge came from talking to the boy by Beaver Rock. Then, making plain that far from inventing the boy and his stolen bed, Andy had been trying to prove them both a hoax, she described the finding of the little skeleton.

The assembled company knew this part of the story; there was a slight rustling and murmuring as Dodie went over it. They all wanted to talk about it some more, Andy could tell—take sides and pick up the party-line debate where they'd left off. Then Dodie told them about the shoe buttons found with the skeleton; that part, they hadn't heard.

"The boy in the tintype," Dodie added casually —but with thunderclap effect—"was also wearing buttoned shoes."

With the suddenly undivided attention of her audience, she went on to the sheriff's entry into the case, introduced Officer Cameron, who was standing quietly by the balcony stair, and explained that the little bones had subsequently been removed to a storage room of the county sheriff's office, where they had to stay until someone with a right to do so claimed them. This, too, was news to most of her listeners. When she said, "My children found this distressing," Andy got a strong impression that a lot of other people agreed, and he saw Kat and Dawnelle exchanging hopeful glances.

Then Dodie went on. "The twins felt they knew this boy, and that he had been sorely abused, and robbed of his resting place. What's more they felt sure he had appealed to them for help, and they had failed him because almost nobody believed what they said. Those who could order the grave opened for investigation"—Dodie carefully did not look at anybody in particular—"have so far been unable to agree."

Another little wave of position shifting and throat clearing passed over the room as she paused.

"Well, I believed them," Dodie went on. "And when they told me what they figured might have happened, back there in early February 1876, I thought they were on the right track. The three of us talked it over, and today I went to Portland to hunt for something to support a sort of theory we developed. I think I found it. First let me explain what we deduced about that long-ago crime."

Carefully, as to a freshman class, she outlined what Andy was beginning to think of as The Peterson Proposition, ticking off the most important points on her fingers and labeling them *A, B, C.*

A. On—or a short time before—February fourth, eighteen seventy-six, a robbery was committed, probably by two persons, somewhere within a fifty-mile radius of Harper's Mill. *B.* The fleeing robbers knew they were pursued and decided to hide what they had stolen. *C.* Stopping for the night in a lonely spot near a little cemetery, they saw a fresh grave—easy to dig up, easy to smooth back to the way they found it, easy to locate later in that back corner with plainly marked gravestones beside and in front of it. *D.* Under cover of dark they removed the dead child from his coffin, put their loot in his place, and hastily reburied his body by stuffing it under a nearby boulder and filling the gap with rock chips and debris. And finally, *E.* For unknown reasons the criminals never returned—unless they did so within a few days of their crime—because once it had settled, the grave was never again disturbed.

"Therefore," Dodie finished, "whatever they put

in that coffin is still there—just as the child's bones were still in their crevice under that rock."

She scanned her classroom sharply, apparently found no really blank faces, then fished in her skirt pocket, produced the Xeroxed page, and drew a long breath. Kat, close at Andy's side, drew one, too. Andy began to hold his.

"Just a minute." Len Harper stood up. "Theory won't hold water. Maybe they did come back a few days later. No way of telling."

"Opening the grave would be a way of telling," Dodie said in a carefully neutral voice.

A voice from the audience, far less neutral, added, "That's what the *meetin's* about!" And another rumbled, "Let 'er finish!"

Mr. Harper hesitated, then sat down.

Dodie said crisply, "I think you'll find there are excellent reasons why those men could not come back." She gestured with the Xeroxed page. "This is a feature article from an *Oregonian* of forty-odd years ago, all about old stagecoach routes and the era of gold mining in Idaho and Eastern Washington. I found it at the Oregon Historical Society, in Portland, in a folder full of clippings about old robberies. I'll read you just one part."

In a room gone tautly silent, she did so.

"Another early-day stagecoach robbery, familiar to pioneers of Sherman County, occurred near The

Dalles on the last day of January eighteen seventy-six. Three thousand dollars in gold dust and a bar of gold bullion were obtained by the bandits. This loot was supposed to have been cached or buried near the scene of the holdup, as it was never recovered, at least officers of Sherman County disclaimed all knowledge of its recovery.

"Two men, Tom Burns and Alex Goodrich, who were known to be 'bad actors' and had been hanging around The Dalles for several days previous to the robbery with no known occupation, were arrested on February seventh, in Sandy, on the west slope of the mountains, as being the highwaymen. They tried to prove an alibi, claiming they were horse buyers newly arrived from southcentral Oregon, waiting to take the stage to Portland and their bank. Both had money belts well filled with twenty-dollar gold pieces.

"Good attorneys were hired in The Dalles to defend them, but they were convicted on the evidence of two Indians who had encountered them in the mountains east—not south—of Sandy three days after the robbery. The Indians, who had gone to meet a relative at a local landmark, came across the two men preparing breakfast and joined them at their campfire.

"When asked in court if anything unusual had occurred while they were at the camp, the Indians stated that a coal of fire had popped out, alighting on the hat of the small man (Goodrich), burning it some before the coal could be thrown off. The hats worn by the men were shown as evidence and on one there was a deep burned scar as indicated by the Indian. The two men were convicted and sentenced to the Oregon Penitentiary, where Goodrich died of tuberculosis. Burns served his term and was released.

"All efforts to get them to divulge the hiding place of their loot were unavailing, both declaring their innocence but hinting that buried treasure might come in very handy some time in the future.

"Burns returned to Sandy after his release, but suddenly disappeared and was never heard of after, or at least by the name of Burns. It was generally supposed that he had recovered his buried loot and disappeared."

Dodie's calm voice stopped. After a moment her riveted listeners came unriveted and began to exchange stares, then whisper, then talk out loud. In thirty seconds the buzz of speculation and argument had become a hubbub, impossible to follow. Andy rolled his eyes at Kat, who was rolling hers at him. He couldn't begin to guess which side was ahead.

"I'm not saying this is proof," Dodie added suddenly, and the room went quiet. "But I find it remarkably suggestive. Do you want me to read it once more, or would you rather ask questions? I realize there are many—uncertain points."

Mrs. Leonard Harper stood up. "Uncertain is right! All they ever proved was that those were the same men the Indians saw, and—"

"Elsa, that's not what we're discussin'," somebody said impatiently. "What *I* wanta know is could they of got up here from The Dalles in just five days—in *winter!*"

Other voices rose. "Story says *'near'* The Dalles. Mighta been twenty miles west—there was a way station at Hood River."

"Yeah, and they musta been horseback. *I* think they done it. I think they robbed that coach."

"But why come all the way up here to dig up a grave! They coulda just dug a hole—"

"Excuse me," Dodie said loudly. To Andy's relief, the conversation stopped. "The highwaymen were convicted and punished. Presumably they were guilty. The question is: Did they hide their loot in that grave? To me, everything points to it. But there's only one way to know for sure."

It was Martin Sweet who stood up this time, cleared his throat, and said, "That's to open the grave. Me and my family reckon we should do it." He stood a moment, then apparently finding nothing to add, sat down.

Leonard Harper popped up. "I want nothin' to do with such un-Christian doings. *I* say we don't!" he retorted.

"This is right where we were at yestiddy!" exclaimed an exasperated voice, echoing Andy's thoughts exactly.

Abruptly, Mrs. Sweet stood up. "But listen here, Len. What's your idea about that little skeleton these kids found? You wanta leave that boy's bones down there in some storeroom? Unburied? You call that Christian? Unless some of us claim 'em they can't be claimed."

"So go on and claim 'em," Leonard retorted before anybody could start a cheer for Mrs. Sweet. He glanced around the room with a cat-ate-the-cream expression. "We'll just make a new grave over in the churchyard cemetery. No use disturbin' an old one just for that."

There was a startled silence, shared by Andy right down to his toes. He was suddenly sure they'd failed. Then from beside him came Kat's voice, shrill and trembling. "No! *No!* You can't! Jacob doesn't want some brand new bed, all in the wrong place, with nobody he knows anywhere around him! *He wants his own.* It was stolen and he wants it back!"

Dodie, who had for the last few minutes been leaning against the fireplace with folded arms and a bemused expression, started toward Kat swiftly. Andy, beside her already, moved close enough to touch the clenched fist pressed against her thigh. *I should've said that,* he was thinking. *Why didn't I say it? I know it as well as she does.* He opened his mouth to say something—anything—but Officer Cameron spoke first.

"Excuse me, folks." A little rustle passed through the room as every head in the place swiveled toward the stairway and the unexpected new voice. Its tone was firm and authoritative; Officer Cameron was at his most official. He stepped forward a few feet from the stairway.

"If there's three thousand dollars worth of gold dust and a bar of bullion cached somewhere between Sandy and The Dalles, I'm interested to find out where. Three thousand in 1876 dollars'll be an awful lot more today, and it most likely belongs to the state. Any chance it's in that grave, sheriff's office'd like to see it opened." He stepped back.

For a minute nobody said a word. Andy could practically hear the cash registers whirring and clashing in almost every brain. Even he knew that a few years ago the price of gold had shot up like Explorer II and never come more than halfway back. Then the room began to buzz. Kat turned to him with her face coming back to life and started to say something, he never knew what, because Leonard Harper was still on his feet and unfortunately still in charge. His nasal voice cut through the rising noise.

"Way I understand it, Officer, sheriff's office can't get that grave opened no matter how interested they are. Not on this kinda old, outa-date crime. Not without the say-so of the cemetery administrators. Izzat right?"

Officer Cameron stared at him woodenly. "If there are no living descendants, that's correct."

"Then speakin' for the Harper's Mill Historical Society—"

" 'Scuse me, Len," interrupted another new voice. Mr. Edwin Harper the postmaster rose, too. "I know you're president—but you can't speak for the Society on this. You musta forgotten. We delegated Ellerton Clark caretaker of that cemetery five years ago, and turned the whole thing over to him. He's got the deciding vote."

The chatter burst out full volume. Kat was squeaking joyously, "I knew it! I told you! But you said he only cut the grass, and chased off the dogs, and—" Andy, remembering Ellerton's refusal to get involved, was trying to catch Mr. Buckle's eye. But he was looking at Ellerton, and in just a moment everybody else was, too, because Ellerton slowly stood up. In the sudden silence, as tranquil as when he was watching his ducks, he spoke in his muted, unemphatic voice.

"I'd ruther somebody else decided. But if I hafta, I will. I don't think anybody here wants to disturb the dead, any more'n Len Harper does. But I don't believe there's anybody in that grave to disturb. I say we take out whatever's there and give that little boy back his bed."

He sat down, and the noise erupted. Leonard Harper shouted over it, got some listeners, and did some vigorous protesting. But pretty soon he was talking to himself.

CHAPTER TWENTY

Andy went to bed in a state of jubilation. He waked at dawn with only one thought in his mind: *What if we're wrong?*

It colored the whole world battleship gray. He pulled on some clothes, ate his breakfast, made a strenuous effort to appear normal. At seven o'clock, he climbed in the car with Dodie and Kat and they drove to the Buckles'. Officer Cameron was there already, waiting with Mr. and Mrs. Buckle and Ellerton on the porch. Five minutes later a sky-blue pickup bounced into the barnyard and the four Sweets climbed out. Leonard and Elsa Harper arrived before the dust had settled, and they brought Reverend Mahaffey. Andy fervently hoped that was all. If he was going to be publicly disgraced and humiliated he wanted as few witnesses as possible.

It had been Officer Cameron's strong advice last night that the grave be opened immediately, without a word about it on the party line; he had arranged it himself, in a series of murmurs, as the meeting was breaking up. Except for the Reverend, whose presence Len Harper had insisted on for the sake of the dead they were going to disturb, the secret seemed to be intact—so far.

"We're all here," said Officer Cameron matter-of-factly. "Let's go."

He picked up a couple of shovels leaning against the porch steps, and started toward the lane. Ellerton followed with the tarpaulin and the two spades, which he had sharpened to brightness on the cutting edge. He's remembering that clover, thought Andy, swallowing hard as he and Kat fell in behind the others. Nobody said anything. Nobody but Officer Cameron had ever done anything like this before. All the others, Andy was suddenly certain, were wondering how they'd ever got into it and wishing themselves on Mars.

And it was *his* fault that they were here instead, picking their way over the dewy mat of clover in the chill of morning to that weathered little stone column half under the blackberry vines. Entirely his fault, when you came right down to it.

He peered back toward the lane, dreading to see a trail of dust that would mean the gathering was no longer private. But the air was blue and clear, the firs on the hillside sketched in ink against it. When he turned back, Ellerton had made the first cut through the clover with one of the sharpened spades. J.B., standing opposite, lined up the other, and shoved it deep with his foot. Methodically they cut a rectangular outline in front of the little stone, then marked out blocks of turf and began to remove them, one by one, and lay them out on the tarpaulin. The spades made little whispering, scraping noises; the diggers occasionally grunted. J.B. paused and took off his jacket. It was hard work.

Andy had wanted to do it. He'd felt he should. Officer Cameron had ruled otherwise, and Mr. Buckle had backed him up. But it would have been easier than waiting. He couldn't quit remembering that it was he, Andy Peterson, who had started the whole thing, that first afternoon—just by stopping to talk to Jacob; he who had kept boring away until he'd convinced Kat and Mr. Buckle and Dawnelle and Dodie, all the people who had gone to bat for him, that Jacob was real and pleading for help. And if they were to find some other long-dead little skeleton in this grave, it was him, Andy Peterson, they were going to blame for being made to look like a bunch of fools.

Andy took a long, quavering breath and wondered if he was going to be able to stand here for whatever time it took to prove him right or wrong.

He became aware that Kat was looking up at him, and met her eyes, which were diagnosing— correctly, he was sure—what was going on inside him right now. She was pale but tranquil. She had got past her worst spot last night, shrieking her mind to Len Harper about Jacob's bed, right out in front of everybody and at the top of her voice. Saying what *I* should have said, thought Andy. Maybe if I'd said it, I'd be feeling now the way she looks.

He swept a self-conscious glance around the circle of faces, wondering if he was looking the way he felt. It didn't matter. Everybody's attention was on the grave.

The clover was all on the tarpaulin now, in shaggy twelve-inch cubes—dark, moist earth on the bottom, threaded with roots, the bunchy green on top like St. Patrick's Day frosting on enormous brownies. Ellerton and J.B. were beginning on the second layer, where the going was easier and fast. It seemed astonishingly fast, all of a sudden, as if Andy had dropped off for a few minutes and awakened to find the men already standing in the grave-pit to work. The more they dug, the faster they seemed to go, and as it turned out, Jacob had not been buried deep. Ellerton was only thigh-deep in the neat, rectangular hole when one of the shovels struck wood.

Both diggers stopped. There was a strange little stir among the watchers, and Dawnelle suddenly whirled and walked quickly over to the Corey section of the cemetery and sat down on one of the old stones with her back turned.

Ellerton spoke to nobody in particular, in his usual serene, muted tones. "We guessed about right on the dimensions, looks like. No need to take the whole coffin out. We'll have the lid clear in a minute and you can just open it up."

And unbelievably, prosaically, just as if it were something people might do any day, that's what Martin Sweet and Officer Cameron did do, a few minutes later. Armed with screwdrivers and crowbars, they stepped cautiously into the hole beside the exposed coffin lid as Ellerton and J.B. hoisted themselves out, and opened it up.

Their tools were scarcely needed. The wood was rotten, the screws mostly rust; the lid came off in two ragged strips. Leonard Harper, standing at the graveside with his captive Reverend beside him, said harshly, "Shall we pray?"

The Reverend Mahaffey even cleared his throat to start. But he got no farther, because as Officer Cameron lifted the second piece of lid away he stood aside, his gaze moving to Andy and a slow smile curving his lips.

As everybody could now plainly see, there was no little skeleton in the coffin. There were only two small metal boxes that had once been enameled black.

Andy took one long, thankful look at them, then returned Officer Cameron's grin with his spirits rising like a sail. Beside him, Kat made some inarticulate little noise and flung her arms around Dodie.

The boxes held ten small, stained, wash-leather sacks containing several ounces of gold dust each, and one shining, slope-sided bar about the size of a thin brick, along with the bill of lading for the shipment, well preserved inside the airtight, moistureproof metal. The bill was dated January 29, 1876, and revealed that the gold had been on its way from a mining company's offices in Pendleton, Oregon, to a San Francisco bank. There were traces of old-fashioned fancy lettering on the boxes' lids that had once spelled out *Cayuse Creek Mines, Walla Walla, Washington.*

The mining company no longer existed. The bank no longer existed. The stagecoaches had long since ceased to run. A proper legal search would of course be made, but it was likely that the recovered gold—now worth not $3,000 but fifteen times that—would revert eventually to the state. Officer Cameron would probably get a medal and a promotion at the very least.

All this information reached the Petersons by ten o'clock that same morning, phoned to the Lodge by Officer Cameron, who had first taken a picture of the boxes still in the grave—he called it *in situ*—then taken charge of the proceedings, and finally taken the boxes themselves away to the sheriff's office in his official car. The grave, on his orders, was left open.

Also on his orders several other things happened —he phrased them as suggestions, but they were welcomed as commands by the bemused little group of those most concerned, all of whom looked as out of their depth as Andy felt.

First, everyone went to the Buckles' house and drank coffee and got back to feeling a little less disjointed and more like going on with the day. Then everybody who didn't live there went home— except Andy, who went out to the barn with Mr. Buckle and Ellerton and helped locate some suitable scraps of cedar left over from Ellerton's office remodeling, then helped build a new little coffin to fit Jacob's bed.

They were just finishing the lid when Kat came down from the Lodge to report what Officer Cameron had told Dodie when he called. This was relayed to the Sweets and Harpers—on the party line—by Mrs. Buckle, who then resignedly took up her old position by the kitchen phone.

On receiving her call, Martin Sweet collected Leonard Harper, then drove to the Buckles' and loaded the new cedar coffin—lined with one of Mrs. Buckle's old quilts—into the back of the sky-blue pickup. The two of them set off with it to Oregon City to make formal claim to the little skeleton and effect its rescue from the hateful evidence property room.

That afternoon—at just about the hour that Andy had first seen Jacob—everybody who had been at the grave in the early morning assembled there again, this time joined by everybody from Harper's Mill who could make it. It was quite a gathering—but to Andy's relief it was a subdued one. The little quilt-lined coffin with its occupant was lowered into the waiting grave, and Reverend Mahaffey got to say his prayer.

Then Ellerton and J.B. restored the dirt from the tarpaulin to its hole, packed it down, and replaced the chunks of clover-woven turf on top. This time Andy got to help. It was the most soul-satisfying, sore-healing work he had ever done. It was like being thirsty for days and days, and finally finding a creek. It was like going without sleep for years and years, and finally getting to rest.

CHAPTER TWENTY-ONE

Three days after Jacob got back his bed, Andy
and Kat stood again in the blackberry-draped
corner of the cemetery, checking on the new
little grave stretching forward from the old little
stone. It was coming along nicely—the mound beginning to settle, the cracks between the chunks
of clover blurring and filling in. The rain last
night had helped. There was supposed to be more
tomorrow.

Today, however, was scoured cloudless by a
warm east breeze, and the sun was high and brilliant. It would probably get hot by mid-afternoon.
Right now it was perfect.

Everything was perfect, at this exact moment—
so it seemed to Andy, and apparently to a blackbird on the iron fence nearby who was telling the
world about it in his liquid whistle. Even the hillside clearing around Beaver Rock had lost its
derelict, lonesome look; he and Kat had both
noticed as they came down the path. It was all right
again, and just looked like a normal piece of hillside
with a big rock sticking up.

"We better go on," Kat said, snapping off her tape and hanging her earphones around her neck. She gave the clover-packed mound a final satisfied appraisal. "It looks just fine, doesn't it?"

"Yeah. Great. Won't take long for that clover to all grow together."

"Dawnelle's roses have wilted, though." Kat reached over and plucked the drooping bouquet from the fruit jar in front of the stone and disposed of them over the fence. "Later on I'll bring down some of our daisies."

"Jacob won't care if you do or not. He'll be asleep. I hope."

"I hope so, too." Kat paused. "I wonder if he's asleep right now, or if it'll take him a while to sort of—get comfortable?"

"I dunno," said Andy. But as Kat started picking her way over the clovery mattress to the gate, he hung back, and—feeling a little silly—whispered, "Good night, Jacob. Sleep tight."

He actually listened a moment, feeling even sillier. And he *almost* thought he heard the answering murmur of a husky, drowsy little voice—but maybe it was only the breeze, rustling through the blackberry tangle.

It didn't matter. Andy didn't care, now, whether the little voice was real or unreal or just the wind passing by. His conscience was clear, his thoughts and stomach on an even keel, and his skies un-troubled, the way he liked them.

Besides that, he and Kat were on their way down to the Buckles' to spend the whole afternoon driving Bonnie and Clyde.